Other Books by Harold Jaffe:
Dos Indios (novel)
Mourning Crazy Horse (stories)
Mole's Pity (novel)
R.M. Bucke's "Walt Whitman" (A Critical Edition)
The American Experience: A Radical Reader (co-editor)
Affinities: A Short Story Anthology (co-editor)

about *Beasts*:

"Man's beastly nature might be an accepted fact, but not even Kafka expressed it with Harold Jaffe's haunting precision. At times surreal, at times overtly political, these stories force us to re-examine our most basic human instincts."

> Rochelle Ratner
> Editor
> *American Book Review*

"Harold Jaffe . . . is one of those few whose fiction deals with what really matters at this juncture in history. *Beasts* is a prime example."

> Hans Koning

"At a time when other short story writers are being praised and petted for their artful ability to say less and less, Harold Jaffe's *Beasts* arrives as a revelation. Here are fictions that *open* doors, admitting light onto our darkest, most accurate dreams of who we are, where we live, what we live, what we must do."

> Fred Pfeil
> Fiction Editor
> *Minnesota Review*

"Jaffe's vision of our social realities is lucid, powerful and inescapably frightening. Given the great compassion from which it springs and toward which it leads us, it is also, with equal force, sacramental. Since the publication of *Mourning Crazy Horse* in 1982—one of the best, most inventive books of stories in recent years—I've considered him to be among our most serious and honorable writers."

> James Baker Hall

BEASTS

fictions by
Harold Jaffe

CURBSTONE PRESS

Several of these fictions were published in
New Directions (Annual), *Boundary 2,*
Fiction International, the minnesota review,
and *American Mode.*

for Jim Scully

printed in the U.S. by
Inter-Collegiate Press
Typeset by YOUR TYPE

Cover design by Deborah Small

ISBN: 0-915306-52-2 (paper)
ISBN: 0-915306-58-1 (cloth)

This publication was supported in part by
The National Endowment for the Arts
and The Connecticut Commission on the Arts,
a State agency whose funds are recommended
by the Governor and appropriated by the
State Legislature.

distributed by
The Talman Company, Inc.
150 Fifth Ave. room 514
New York, NY 10011

published by
CURBSTONE PRESS
321 Jackson Street, Willimantic, CT 06226

BEASTS

ONE

GIRAFFE

The rain had just about stopped when I went into the barber shop. He was cutting a child's hair, the child raised up on two cushions on the barber's chair. I sat on a folding chair and leafed through PENTHOUSE. The barber was finishing, dusting the child's neck with talc, removing the tissue bib and linen sheet, lifting the child to the floor. The child's mother—I hadn't seen her until that moment—a slight woman, oddly coarse-featured, paid the barber and they left. The barber then went through the curtain into the back of the shop. I heard the toilet flush and the water tap come on. When he returned I was sitting where the child had sat.

He was drying his hands with a towel—he stopped and glared at me:

"What do you want here?"

"What do I want? I want a haircut."

He looked chagrined, even revolted. His eyes bulged:

"I won't cut your hair. No way. Now get out of here."

I couldn't believe this. He had cut my hair a dozen times before. I didn't know what to say.

"But you know me," I said.

He was shaking his head vehemently and even picked up the phone—his hand was trembling with rage.

"If you don't leave this second I'll—"

I got up out of the chair, left.

13

Coming down hard again, harder than before. I ducked into a nearby doorway. I still couldn't believe what happened. What the hell was wrong with him? Though he'd never been chatty-friendly the way some barbers are, he'd always been polite. The street was deserted. It was a quarter to seven. I decided to run for it. This didn't help—it was pouring and I had too far to go. I turned the corner and ducked into a small lighted storefront. It was another barbershop, very small. I went inside. An elderly black man in a long white bib-apron stepped forward.

"Haircut, young sir?" in a soft voice.

"Well . . ."

He made a ceremonial dusting-off motion on the single barber's chair and gestured to me, smiling.

I removed my sopping jacket, draped it on the back of one of the three folding chairs then fitted myself into the raised leather barber's chair.

He attached the tissue bib to my neck than draped the white long cloth about me.

"Haircut and shave, young sir?" softly, smiling.

"No shave, thanks. Just a haircut. I wouldn't know myself without a beard."

"The beard becomes you, young sir."

"Oh. Thanks."

He had begun to use comb and scissors on my rain-wet hair.

I was looking around for something to read, didn't see magazines or newspaper. But then he put something in my hand, a small dog-eared paperback without its cover, without a title page. It began on page 14 with the syllable "ly."

> ly acacia but while the giraffe nibbled
> she was killed shot in the side at once
> blood gushed like an artesian well like
> an underground oil well in Texas she lay
> on her side with her eyes open an acacia
> sprig in her mouth they were after the
> tip of the tail the brush part considered

an aphrodisiac would fetch $$$ in hamburg
tokyo paris new york

No title, no author. No punctuation. I couldn't make it
out. I glanced in the soiled mirror at the barber, attentively
snipping my hair: a slender, trim-looking man with white
hair, white mustache, in his sixties probably.
"Have you been here for a while?" I asked.
"I don't follow, sir."
His speech sounded as much Caribbean as American,
though not distinctly like either.
"Your shop," I said. "I don't recall noticing it before."
He laughed at this, an odd full-throated laugh. Odd, be-
cause I didn't see how what I said provoked it.
"Strong thick hair," he said.
"Mine?"
He nodded, smiling.
"I think I'm beginning to lose a little, from the left side."
"Uh-huh," still smiling, nimbly working scissors and
comb.
The rain had diminished, but now picked up again. I
heard it pelting the window.
"I hope it lets up before too long," I said.
"What's that, young sir?"
"The rain."
He nodded again. An impressive-looking head (I was
looking at him in the mirror), more African and vigorous
than I had noticed before. Small ears close to his head;
broad, high cheekbones; fleshy sculpted nose and lips; clear
deep-set eyes under his glasses. I was looking at the words
in the book again:

great thrust of the heart that delivers
blood to the head gushing now blood through
the wide bullet hole in her side near
the heart the killers each on one knee
with their machetes on the vivid plain

15

why murder the eighteen-foot two-ton
animal for the fourteen-inch brush at the
end of her tail it is quicker this way
the brush will fetch $$$ gushing tokyo
paris hamburg new york

No punctuation anyplace. I looked up again, through the
mirror, at the barber.

"What's the name of this shop?"

"You want the shop's name or my name?"

"All right, your name then."

"My name is Quitus."

"Q-u-i-t-u-s?"

"Correct, sir," continuing to snip, hair raining onto my
sheet.

"Your shop doesn't have the barber's pole outside, does
it?"

"Not at all, young sir." He laughed that same throaty bass
laugh.

I turned back to the book, but then looked up again.

"What time do you close?"

"I was closed when you came in," the barber—Quitus—
said. "So I opened. When you're gone I'll close again."

I didn't know how to take this. My face didn't look the
same in the mirror. Because of the play of light, my wet hair,
maybe the mirror itself, the contours of my face didn't look
the same.

"Are you alone, young sir?"

"Alone? Do you mean am I married?"

Quitus shrugged his shoulders.

"I'm not married," I said.

He said, "Ah."

I was looking in the mirror at the bearded youngish white
in the white sheet being tended to by the slender old black
in the white apron. I turned back to the book:

acacia leaves from one of the upper branches
while her calf ate acacia leaves from a
lower branch acacia horrida horrida because
of the violence of the thorns which do not
trouble the giraffe though she grasps
with her prehensile tongue eighteen inches
long full of blood-filled papillae the
brush must come from the tail of a female
soon after she's birthed to ensure the
potency of the brush say the jobbers
speaking for the users in fact it is not
an aphrodisiac not truly hamburg tokyo
paris new york

"What is this?" I said. "This book?"
We were talking through the mirror.
"How do you find it then?"
"Puzzling. I can't make it out."
He chuckled. "How would you wish it to be?"
"That's just it. If I knew what it was supposed to be—is it
fiction?"
"What's that?"
"Fiction?"
"Yes."
"It's imagined. Made up. Like a novel or a story."
"No."
"It's not fiction?"
"No." He smiled.
I nodded my head slowly. "I was just wondering. It
doesn't have title or author."
"Ah," Quitus said.
"After a minute I said, "You're the second barber I saw
today. The first wouldn't cut my hair."
"Is that so, young sir?"
"Yes. I can't figure it out. He cut my hair on a regular
basis for a year or more, but this time he threw me out of his
shop. Like he didn't know me."
Quitus didn't respond.

"Even not knowing me—why would he act like that? The idea of cutting my hair seemed to . . . disgust him. He actually threatened to phone the police."

Quitus, working scissors and comb, nodded his head slowly.

"Look, I think maybe you're taking too much off, Quitus."

"Not at all, sir. Please do relax."

Quitus tilted the chair back so that I could no longer look into the mirror. I raised the book to my eyes:

>still gushing blood after twenty minutes
>it was an hour after sunup heating up
>on the east african plain the two gunmen
>held machetes impatient now sweating wanting
>to get on with it hack the tail with its
>aphrodisiacal brush hack it free move on
>get at least four brushes today jobbers
>in pretoria in dar es salaam in nairobi
>insisted on the entire tail so as to
>avoid deception though the brush was not
>truly an aphrodisiac demonstrate their
>bona fide to hamburg paris tokyo new york

I laid the book on my chest and closed my eyes. Quitus was working carefully, deliberately. I was feeling, suddenly, chilled from the rain. At that moment he said:

"The young master is chilled," snipping.

I opened my eyes but could not see him either above me or, because of the chair's tilt, through the mirror.

"My name," I said, "is—"

I didn't get it out. The door jingled: someone came into the shop. With Quitus working my head I couldn't move to see, but I heard that he was black. After greeting Quitus he said:

"Cooney—you think he got a chance?"

"Cooney," Quitus said, "ain't got nothin."

"What bothers me is age," the other man said, standing

next to Quitus, above me (I smelled the rain on him).
"Holmes ain't no spring chicken."

"Don't matter what he ain't," Quitus said. "Matter what
he is, and he the heavyweight champeen of the free mother-
fuckin world. What's Cooney?"

Talking with his friend, Quitus sounded like a working-
class black. Diction, pitch, cadence—completely different
from the way he had been talking to me. He was animated,
as was the other man, who was—I smelled it—smoking a
cigar.

"What's Cooney?" Quitus said.

"Cooney ain't nothin."

"That's what I'm sayin."

I heard the other man drag on his cigar, actually felt the
heat of the cigar near my left ear.

"One thing 'bout Cooney," the other man said. "He big."
big."

"Yeah, he big," Quitus said. "But he soft. He 'bout the
softest big white man you gonna see."

All the time he was speaking Quitus kept snipping. I
cleared my throat:

"Quitus, don't take off too much now."

He tapped my cheek reassuringly.

"You know who that Cooney remind me of?" Quitus
said.

"Who that?"

"Carnera. You remember Carnera? Great big mother-
fucker. Fought Joe Louis in the forties. It was a joke."

"Louis got him?"

"Got him!" Quitus snorted. "Louis done et him and spit
him the fuck out. And Carnera was a lot tougher white guy
than this one. Cooney. Weren't as soft."

The other man took a long pull on his cigar and the smoke
went into my eye. I tried to shift my head but couldn't—
Quitus had a restraining hand on my shoulder.

"Now I ain't sayin Holmes be as tough as Joe Louis,"
Quitus said.

"Thas right."

"Fak is he don't have to be all that tough cause this Cooney don't have nothin a'tall."

The other man chuckled. "If I had me some money—"

Quitus: "You'd put it on the brother, right?"

"You better believe it." He laughed, then touched palms with Quitus.

"Look, I got to split. You take care, heah?"

"You do the same," Quitus said.

The door opened, the man left.

Quitus straightened the chair. I looked at myself in the mirror.

"Well, young sir?"

"It's fine. A little short maybe."

"Not at all. It is still raining quite hard. Are you in a hurry?"

"Hurry? I guess not."

"Shall I trim the beard?"

"All right, but not too much."

Quitus smiled. He tilted the chair again so that I was on my back, then handed me the book.

crouched on one knee machetes blood still
gushing had formed a small pool of blood
commenced to flow toward them down-grade
slightly didn't notice till it soiled their
boots and knees on the ground they shifted
irritated it was taking so long wanting to
get on with it hack it free fetch more much
more than truffles than rhino's horn in
paris tokyo hamburg new york

Quitus was humming. It sounded like "Amazing Grace." I laid the book down on my lap.

"And how long have you had your beard, young sir?"

"Ever since I got out of the service—about four years."

"It certainly suits the young master," Quitus said.

"Please don't call me young . . . "

Quitus had moved toward the sink and turned on the tap. He continued to hum. Then he was back and I felt a wet hot towel on my face.

"This feels very nice, does it not? It will cut the chill, sir. The chill you picked up outside in the rain. After you had been denied by the other barber. Who refused to touch your hair. Denied for no reason that you can understand. As if suddenly, with your hair and face wet, the play of the light, you were not yourself. Someone else. No explanation. Forced out of his shop into the rain. Where you picked up your chill."

Quitus pronounced these odd sentences in a soft monotone. I lay there with my face swathed in a wet hot towel. I felt like someone who had received a head injury in a war. Who was in the process of becoming someone else.

"Was he your friend?" I asked, my voice muffled from under the wet towel. "The other man who came in here and talked to you about boxing?"

"Ah, the young master likes boxing."

"Well, I don't have any special feeling for boxing. But I've read about the fight, Cooney-Holmes. It's hard to keep from reading about it."

"I think that the young master does not care for blood sports." He was patting my face with the towel.

"Please don't call me that, Quitus. My name is Stu."

"Very good, sir."

Silence. I closed my eyes. I felt suddenly sleepy. Quitus patted and massaged my face.

"They're billing Cooney as another Rocky," I said. "You know 'Rocky,' the movie?"

"Uh-huh."

"Dumb sentimental crap," I said. "Racist."

"Uh-huh," massaging my face.

Quitus removed the towel from my face, picked up his comb and a smaller pair of scissors and began to trim my mustache. He was humming "Amazing Grace" again, softly.

When he finished with the mustache he exchanged small scissors for larger scissors, then picked up the book which had fallen on the floor, shook the hair from it, handed it to me.

> with the force of erupting lava except
> red very red through the jagged hole in
> her left side she lay on her right side
> with her eyes open on the killing and
> selling side they of course knew it wasn't
> an aphrodisiac the fourteen inch brush
> at the tip of the long tail of the eighteen-
> foot two-ton ruminant and they knew that
> the users the wealthy consumers knew in
> hamburg paris tokyo new york

I set down the book. "So you get enough customers to keep your barbershop a going concern?" I asked pointlessly. Quitus was trimming my beard.

He chuckled. "Every gentleman has to get a haircut, young sir. And some gentlemen they like to get a nice shave too, a pleasant face-massage. Soothing. Isn't that the truth, young sir?"

I nodded.

"You see, if Quitus doesn't do it someone else will. Or it could also be that if Quitus doesn't do it nobody else will. Do you understand what I'm saying, young sir? Stu?"

I said I did. I closed my eyes.

Quitus was now whistling "Amazing Grace."

I opened my eyes and looked again at the book, turning the pages: all of it written the same way, without punctuation, without pause, all about the killing of a female giraffe, whose blood gushed to the ground with enormous force, while the killers impatiently waited with their machetes to sever the tail, so as to present the terminal brush to jobbers, who would then market it in Tokyo, Paris, Hamburg and New York for big money, because the brush was supposed to be an aphrodisiac, but in fact wasn't, and evidently everyone knew it wasn't . . .

"Do you, young sir, cry out in passion?"

I closed the book and set it in my lap. "What did you say, Quitus?"

"I asked whether you cried out in passion?"

"You mean . . ."

"Thas right."

Pause.

"I do," I said haltingly. "Sometimes. Other times, no. It's not something," I said, "that comes easy for me."

Pause.

"What makes you ask?" I said.

Quitus slipped the comb and scissors into his breast pocket and picked up a hand-mirror from the shelf, set the chair upright, rotated it 180 degrees, held up the mirror behind my head, then to either side of my beard.

"Fine," I said. "Very good."

Quitus rotated the chair so that I was facing the mirror again, picked up a brush from the counter, poured talc on it. He loosened my bib and dusted my neck.

"That brother you was askin about," he said. "That was in heah before?"

"Who was talking with you about the Cooney-Holmes fight, you mean?"

"Thas right."

Quitus and I were looking at each other through the mirror. I looked shorn and older somehow. He looked different too: standing with his weight on one leg in a kind of jive, street-wise way, his eyes suddenly glazed.

"That brother be blind," Quitus said. "You dint know that, did you?"

"No. Blind? I didn't hear him use a cane or anything."

Quitus snorted. "He don't use none of that. You know why he blind?"

I shook my head.

"He blind cause he do like what I ast you. He called out in passion. Except you say you can't do it easy and you ain't black. He called out in passion wit his woman, and he called

23

out in passion wit de way things is in de world. You understand what I'm sayin?"

Pause.

"I'm not sure."

Quitus gave a short sardonic laugh or grunt. He picked up the giraffe book from my lap and set it on the counter. Then he removed the bib from my neck and the sheet from my body. He shook the sheet twice, folded it, laid it on the counter.

I made to get up but he had a hand on my shoulder.

"Did the brother come acrost like he was a little slow?"

We were still talking through the mirror.

"I don't know, Quitus. He's blind and slow too?"

This time Quitus laughed louder.

"I told you he was a man cried out in his passion. Well, he weren't blind then, and he weren't slow. He was head-quick and real mad at shit and so straight-out wit his passion, dat they blinded him. You dig? And they beat his head in so bad dat he lost all quickness. You dig?"

He was glaring at me through the mirror.

"And you," he said, "want to know what it's all about. What it's all about is the brother dat they couldn't strip his passion they done killed it *in* him and damn near killed him too. I reckon they oughta have, since he ain't but a shell of what he was."

I didn't know what to say. Again I tried to stand up and Quitus held me by the shoulder.

"He—your friend—didn't seem all that slow to me," I said.

Quitus laughed. "Who you? A young white man wit a young beard on yo face. Whatchoo know about *seem?*"

Pause.

This time I managed to get up out of the chair. I removed my wet jacket from the back of the folding chair and put it on. Then I turned to him.

"How much do I owe you?"

For the first time since I had come into the shop we were

24

actually looking at each other, not through the mirror. Quitus really was slight, elderly. Almost transparent in his white bib-apron. And now his manner had changed back to how it had been.

"How much do I owe you, Quitus?"

"Four dollars even, young sir. And you'd better get going quick, before the rain starts up again."

I paid him, zippered up my wet jacket, and opened the door.

"Goodbye, Quitus," I said and closed the door.

I had walked only ten or fifteen yards when I pivoted and went back to Quitus' shop. I tried the door but it was locked. Quitus, bent over the sink washing his hands, looked up and saw me at the door. He didn't seem surprised, nor did he move toward the door to open it. I got down on my knees and pushed my head up against the mail slot.

"Quitus," I shouted. "Tell me what I should do."

PELICAN

"The Pelican is greatly devoted to its young and,
finding them in the nest killed by snakes, tears at
its breast, bathing them with its blood to bring
them back to life."

Leonardo da Vinci
(Quoted in J.L. Borges'
The Book of Imaginary Beings)

We did it for about a year and a half, okay? The real stuff, I
mean. Before that we like did it with another pair two, three
times. The same pair, people we knew. And it was pretty
good. We—Burt and me—had went a little flat and getting it
on with this pair it helped us. We got our edge back. But
then after a while we went flat again.

"Flat?"

Yeah. I mean we balled and stuff, just there wasn't much
zip to it. Burt and I been married almost nine years and we
couldn't like uncover anything new about each other. Each
other's body. So we talked about maybe getting into swinging to like see how it was. Either that or separating for a
while.

"Why didn't you just separate for a while?"

It's a hassle. We have a joint savings account and stocks. Plus life insurance. We have a real good insurance policy but it depends on us living in the same household. And there are the kids. Besides, we still kind of loved each other, okay? So we sent away for this swingers magazine that has photos and phone numbers and stuff. We went through it real careful making a check next to the ads that appealed to us. We were a little nervous about it, but it was a turn-on too. Just going through the ads got us feeling real sexy and we got it on like right there, on the carpet. Few days later we sent replies to two of the ads from Central Jersey where we live.

"What sort of replies?"

What sort? Photos. Not nude photos—we didn't have any nude photos of ourselves then. Photos, details about our age, jobs, family, what we liked to do in sex. Like I'm bi but Burt isn't. We wrote that. Anyways, one of the parties responded and the other didn't. This isn't unusual. We found out later that half or more of the swingers you wrote to didn't respond for one reason or another. But the party that did respond were interested. They were about our age, pretty nice people, and the woman—her name was Joan— was real sexy, petite and delicate, very graceful. Which needless to say turned my husband on. Joan's husband—I think his name was Stan—wasn't all that much, kinda overweight, not at all like his photo. But he was friendly and he was hung nice and when we got down to it he knew how to get it on.

"What was the sequence that first time? How did you get into it—do you remember?"

Yeah, I do. Lot of other times are jumbled together in my memory even though some of them were real sexy. But this one, being it was the first, I remember all of it. The etiquette is when you respond to a published ad, you have first choice about where you meet. And we wanted to do it at our place thinking it would be easier there. Joan and Stan—no, his name was Stew, short for Stewart—they didn't mind. So we sent the kids to Burt's mother on the shore for the weekend, and Joan and Stew came by around ten o'clock on a Friday night. What was the sequence? We talked, drank some of this strong sweet liqueur called Chartreuse, which they had brought over. It's supposed to be a kind of turn-on, I guess. We shared a joint too. Things were moving kind of slow, we were still dressed, and to tell you the truth I was feeling a little like the whole thing was a mistake and not at all turned-on, when Stew suggested Burt take his wife into our bedroom. Burt went for the idea and so did Joan. While they were in the bedroom Stew and I did a little bit, not much. Touched each other, talked. Then after a while we went into the bedroom where Joan and Burt were into it pretty good. We took our clothes off and joined in.

"And you saw this couple—Joan and Stew—again?"

We saw them once more about a month later. Also at our place. It was okay. Not super. Burt really was turned on by Joan, like I said. And I didn't blame him, I liked her too. But Stew, in spite of being a good technician, didn't do it for me. Besides, we were into a few other things by then which were pretty interesting. There were other pairs, and there was this single, an olive-skinned girl from Trinidad. Her name was Lakshmi, real pretty, bi and turned on by just about anything. Lakshmi was perfect for us because we were still a little unsure of ourselves and our technique.

"What do you mean turned on by anything? Like what, for instance?"

Well, for instance Greek. Lakshmi had a great ass, and she dug enemas, she dug being butt-fucked. We swung with Lakshmi maybe six, seven times, and it was only like

29

the last few times that we found out she was into bondage, rubber, the whole S&M scene. The next-to-last time we saw her she came with a guy, young, maybe gay. All he wanted was Lakshmi to whip his ass and Lakshmi—in rubber and six-inch spike-heels—really did it to him. We all got off on it. I'll tell you what: if we had had a big male dog Lakshmi would have made it with him. She was a regular sex machine.

"You and Burt never made it with an individual male?"

Never. I kinda wanted to try it. Lots of male singles advertised in the magazine, and sometimes we'd meet a guy at a party or something that turned me on. But Burt couldn't handle it. Like I said before, he isn't bi, so he wouldn't be able to do much besides share me with another guy, which he didn't really want to do. I never made a big deal over it. The pair scene was good, the occasional female single thing was good, and me and Burt were in a real nice groove together. Until that first thing happened.

"When was that?"

About five, six months after we got into it. It was going good pretty much. Not that we didn't have some clinkers, and there were a couple of times when the other people thought us, or one of us, were clinkers too. But then we were pretty heavy into it, two and three times a week a lot of times, and also we were doing larger scenes, two, three other pairs and more.

"What's a clinker?"

Rejection. That's your commonest clinker. I've seen like real beautiful chicks and guys rejected, okay? I mean everybody has their own head, that's the way it is. Another clinker is banging your own drum, forcing your own shit on someone that doesn't want it. Which is what happened to me. We were with two other pairs in Danbury, Connecticut—we weren't sticking only to Jersey anymore. One of the pairs was okay but I saw right off that the other pair was weird. The woman was like stoned on Quaaludes or something, she was kinda nodding out. The guy—he was a stocky aggressive dude with long dirty hair, like a biker. And he had eyes only for me. My instinct told me to like cut out, but Burt sort of liked the woman from the other pair, and the guy from this pair was kind of sexy. So we stayed and we got into it, all of us except the biker's woman who was sort of laying there. Well, the biker started really coming on. I don't mind rough, but not his kind of rough. Right off he took hold of my head and forced me down on him, like he thought he was down on the docks with a queer or something. Then he tried to butt-fuck me, and when I pulled away he slapped me around. We were in a big wide room and Burt was busy in another part of it. But when I started to scream Burt and the guy from the other pair came over and tried to pull the prick away from me. But then he went really crazy and attacked Burt, hitting him in the face with his fists, trying to kill him it seemed like. This went on for like a long time, the dude had pinned Burt to the floor and was beating the life out of him. It was weird because while he was slamming Burt he was silent, not making a sound. The rest of us were screaming, trying to separate them, but this mother was too strong, too fucking crazy. Finally he just stopped, got up, put on his pants, grabbed his nodding bitch, and left.

"When did this happen?"

What's this? December? It was in the summer. The summer before this last one. Burt's nose was broke and both of his eyes were badly bruised. But worse than that, he was really messed up inside. Getting beat up bad like that under those circumstances got him real down on himself. He didn't want to see people anymore, started saying these super moral things about how bad it is to make it with other people and stuff. He wasn't even making it with me, his wife. I didn't push him because I knew it was a terrible thing, the whole thing that happened was terrible. It just wasn't good for him to be so down on himself, so guilty. But no matter how supportive I tried to be, it hurt us. It hurt our relationship, and we were even talking again of separating for a while. We were both real down, I can tell you, and the kids naturally were picking up on it too. And then we heard from Rory and Roy.

"They wrote?"

No, phoned. If they had wrote we wouldn't have answered. Not the way we were feeling. They had seen our ad in a back issue of the magazine and Rory phoned. It must've been a couple of months after that other thing had happened and things between Burt and I were at an all-time low. He usually slept in the day-bed in the living room. Sometimes he didn't come home at nights, and a few times I didn't either. The kids were grumpy. The only reason we didn't actually split up was what I mentioned before. Anyways, it was a weekday night, Burt was helping Carol, our youngest, with her homework, and I was doing my nails in the bathroom. The phone rang and Burt answered it. From the bathroom I could hear him talking and listening and then talking again, and something in his voice told me it was an unusual phone call, a good call. I sort of heard his voice change from grumpy and depressed to interested and charming, like his old self. I was wondering what the hell was going down when he called me: "Baby, I'd like you to talk with someone." He sure hadn't called me baby in a long time. I got on the phone while Burt picked up the extension in our bedroom. Soon as I heard Rory talk for a little bit, I understood how she had gotten to Burt.

"What was it? Something in her voice?"

Something in *her*. Her voice, her way of holding herself, everything she did, really, showed what she was. I found this out later when we got to know Rory. But then, listening and talking with her on the phone, there was something sincere and open about her. Burt and I both felt friendly, at home with her, right off. We must've been on the phone forty-five minutes and I can't tell you now what we talked about—besides getting together, that is. She and her husband wanted Burt and I to get together with them. We said that we had kinda stopped swinging, and Rory suggested that we talk about it together and let her know. Not only did Burt and I talk about it, we made love for the first time in a long time and it was great. We saw Rory and Roy for the first time the following Saturday at their place. A real cute place on the Jersey shore. Rory answered the door and she looked pretty much the way I expected. Real attractive, tall and slender, with long wavy auburn hair, in her early thirties. Another thing I noticed which didn't surprise me when I thought about it was her scent. Instead of perfume or cologne, she smelled of talc, a real fresh scent. She led us into the living room where three other people were sitting and talking, a pair about our age and a man who looked to be in his forties in a wheelchair. That was Roy. I remember that Burt and I looked at each other, wondering.

"How did Roy respond to you?"

He smiled and held out his left hand. He had a very sweet smile. He used his left to shake hands because the right side was where most of the damage was. He explained this to us in a very direct, quiet sort of way, while we were all sitting there having a drink. The other pair—Mack and Joanne—already knew the story. Roy had survived a plane crash about fifteen years ago, but his spinal cord had been damaged and he was a quadraplegic. In his case that meant his right side,

33

legs and arms, was paralyzed. In the past I had always been kind of turned off—scared, I guess—by wheelchairs, but I didn't feel that way about Roy. Still Burt and I were surprised when Rory sat on his lap and they started necking. After a bit, Rory got up and suggested we go into the sunroom, a lovely glassed-in room with plants and pretty rugs and cushions. Rory helped Roy undress and laid him on one of the rugs on his back. He had a pretty nice body, a little soft maybe, but nice skin. He didn't at all look paralyzed. He was hung okay too, about average. He had a nice broad chest. The crazy thing of it was that while I was watching how gentle and easy and sensual Rory undressed him and helped him on to the rug, I got turned on. Mack and Joanne were also getting undressed, and so me and Burt did too. In a while we were all laying around kinda touching each other, almost like kids. Everybody was relaxed and gentle and it was a lot of fun. A while later we got into the adult stuff and it was great, natural and sexy and relaxed.

"Roy was able to perform adequately?"

Roy was fine, except that he depended on Rory to get started. The accident had damaged the nerve endings between his penis and his brain—I don't know if I'm explaining this right. Anyways, he couldn't get an erection by thinking about it, so Rory got him hard by first masturbating then sucking him. Then Joanne sat on his cock, and then I did, and let me tell you something—it was good. He was right there, real alive. That's how he felt to me, like someone half his age but relaxed, gentle. Roy and Rory were bi, and so was Joanne. Mack and Burt held back a little, but after a while they got into it too, everyone was with everyone else and it was great. It was like the best time we had ever had swinging and Burt and I talked about it for a long time afterwards. We didn't know whether it was because we had stayed away for a while, or whether it was the people. For sure they weren't the sexiest people we had been with. They looked good and Rory was beautiful, but it wasn't so much her body that was beautiful as just all of her. Her body was in good shape but she was probably closer to forty than thirty, there were stretch marks on her breasts. But it didn't matter. With Rory the looks thing didn't really matter.

"You saw Rory and Roy again soon after?"

We wanted to see them again real soon, but the thing was they moved around a lot. Mack and Joanne, who we swung with a lot, told us that Rory and Roy had lived in Africa and South America and Hong Kong, I think it was. Like we saw them on Saturday and the following Monday they flew to Mexico, and from there to Guatemala. Mack said he had no idea what Rory and Roy did in these places, except maybe swing. Anyways, we saw them again at their place about three weeks later. Mack and Joanne and a real attractive black pair were there. Sheryl and Joe, the black pair, were having a kind of problem. Joe had hurt his knee real bad and had it operated on and wasn't able anymore to fuck like a cowboy-stud on top of Sheryl, which is the way she liked it. Rory and Roy showed them how good it was, and how varied too, with Joe on his back and Sheryl on top. Like I said, Rory had this simple relaxed way, and she knew how to kid around—she and Roy were always kidding each other. Joe and Sheryl dug the new positions real quick without being uptight, and it was great all around, a long, long session and we didn't have to toke up or snort or anything else to keep it real.

"You said you enjoyed making it with Roy. How was it with Rory?"

Great. I think I said about balling Roy that he was all there. So was Rory. It's hard to describe this feeling, but you must know what I mean. When we—Rory and me—were together, caressing, going down, whatever, there was a

35

sweet steady kind of feeling about it. In scenes people tend to be like on the move—a taste here, a taste there. Rory wasn't like that. Burt agreed with me too, he loved balling Rory. I think he dug balling her more than he did me.

"And that didn't upset you?"

No. Swinging sex is recreational. It's not the same as loving somebody. People who swing say this a lot, maybe too much, but I think it's true. Let's face it, in the year and a half we were into it, there've been guys I really dug balling, but I haven't loved Burt the less for it.

"How many times did you swing with Rory and Roy altogether?"

Just four times. After that they took off again, this time for India and Nepal—that area. They sure picked far-out places to go to, and it must've been a hassle with Roy handicapped and all. Anyways, they said they'd probably be back in a year or so. And it's been almost a year since they left. They sent us a couple of cards, but with no return address. That's about it. We miss them. Me and Burt both miss them.

"You stopped swinging for good?"

Yeah. I think so. We'll see how we feel when Rory and Roy get back. After they left we did it for a while, but it wasn't the same. Then Carol, our youngest, came down with a real bad infection which the doctor thought was spinal meningitis. She was real sick for a long time and we didn't want to leave her. By the time Carol got better—and it took about five months—we had just kinda lost interest. In swinging, I mean.

"Do you still keep in contact with any of the people you swung with?"

Not really. We talked to Mack and Joanne a couple of times, though what we talked about was Rory and Roy. And believe it or not, that weirdo biker that beat up on Burt actually phoned me a couple of months ago. I told him to leave me alone or I would call the cops. He didn't call back.

"And with you and Burt? How does it go?"

So-so. We're hanging in there.

BROTHER WOLF

Molly's in the cramped elevator with dirty yellow walls. It stops abruptly at a lower floor and an old man with a tattered coat and red watchcap pulled low over his ears steps inside. The old man is using his thumb to rub the opaque film from his lottery ticket. His hands tremble. The elevator stops again and a pale man with a nervous manner steps in. Runs a pocket comb through his thin dry hair.

Rain outside. Molly waits to cross the Artery. White cars, long trucks. She waits but can't get across. Has to walk to the overpass. Beneath the overpass, near one of the buttresses, V's OD'd again, sprawled on the pavement, coupla kids bent to him.

Leaning against the railing on the overpass, Loraine and F are fixing. Loraine has a yellow leatherette belt around her arm. F just got back from the Rack. Molly nods, walking past.

The Artery dips into the tunnel that cuts through the business loop. Molly enters the tunnel, walking on the narrow pedestrian strip. Whoosh of speeding cars, trucks. Exhaust clouds. The strip is full, M is there, Lois.

Lois to Molly, "You have?"

Molly shakes her head no.

"I got coin," Lois says.

"Don't have," Molly says.

Traffic's loud, Lois can't hear.

"Don't have," Molly shouts. "Try Wolf."

"Wolf has?" Lois shouts.

Molly nods.

Kids on the railing, against the tunnel walls. A boy Molly's seen but don't know squeezes her tit, grins. She keeps walking. Magda's going down on a john, squatting on spike heels in one of the shallow doorways. Leni and R are making out against the railing. Both wear headsets, Leni's sort of nodding out.

R says to Molly, "Wolf's shit, real tasty."

Alone against the railing is the Tattoo Prince. Just about everyone has homemades on their bodies, but Prince is full of them, back and front. His face too. He nods.

"Hello, Prince," Molly says, slipping her headset into place. She's into the sounds as she leaves the tunnel. The Artery widens to eight lanes. Still raining. She's just about lost her in. She'll need a boost by the time she gets to P. She turns up the volume.

She's walking on the strip along the Artery to P. It was P's scam and Wolf thought it would work. Scamming Molly's father. Molly thinks of her father as she passes one of his affiliate-buildings, glass and steel, recessed at the center, sort of jutting out at the top. He has a suite in another one just like this, high up, looks out over the city. Her father and mother live apart, but he kinda likes Molly. They hardly ever meet though. Last time was about a year ago in his penthouse suite. He brushed her head and gave her coin. Molly and P were in real tasty with that coin. Not for that long though.

The scam'll keep them in for a long damn time. Except she's needing now and the sounds ain't working either. A john brakes his car and shows coin.

"I won't hump," Molly says.

He nods.

She does him for coin. In his white car on a utility road.

Moving again she sees D who sells her some. She wants to wait for P, do it with him. She don't know if she can wait.

When P mentioned the scam Wolf said, do it. Tap the old man. He makes out he loves his daughter, test him. Will he stick his hand in the vault for his daughter? Will he stick both hands in? Will he stick them in up to his elbows? Let him take a tax writeoff. He must have that stip in his policy, kidnapping loss.

That's Wolf.

Molly smiles. But she is scared a little. Or maybe it's just she's low, needing. She thinks of sticking. Just something till she gets to P. That's what she does. Stops off in a toilet, waits for a stall, sticks some. Others fixing and she thinks, maybe, but she don't have her kit. P has it. So she just sticks some above her wrist. Small boost, hold her till she gets to P.

Still raining. She stops at a newspaper stall and buys a paper that she puts on top of her head. A truck sprays water on her. Someone says her name. Fritz.

"Molly."

"Hey, Fritz."

"Here, girl."

Fritz is away from the rain, sprawled on the pavement, leaning against a building. He just fixed, it's in his eyes. He takes the paper from Molly's head and pulls her down next to him. He starts to read the sopping newspaper aloud, saying words like Circuitry and Private Sector and Network and Exxon and Prayer . . .

Fritz reads these words in an exaggerated way, grinning. Then he says, "I heard. You and P gonna try and scam your old man?"

Molly looks at him.

"What happens if it don't work?"

Molly shrugs.

Fritz grins. "What you got to lose, right?"

Molly nods, gets up, continues walking. Only without the newspaper on her head. Raining kind of hard. She turns up the volume on her headset.

P is waiting for her. They kiss. He looks wasted.

She nods yes before he even asks.

They fix in one of the shooting cellars, use P's works and

Molly's lucky belt. When they use Molly's laminated blue vinyl belt it usually means a tasty in.

This time it don't work all that good, it's an okay in, that's about it.

Leaning against one of the water pipes in the cellar, P says, "Me and Wolf did the letter."

He hands Molly an envelope with her father's name and address on it. Inside, put together from newspaper print:

> We have your daughter Molly and will kill her unless you give us what we demand. Eight hundred thousand dollars must be left in front of Getty Affiliate 3 on East Artery and Seminole. Exactly at six am on Thursday 24 May, the money in a transparent bag should be placed on the concrete step that leads to the generator room on the north side of the building. We will be in touch with you again soon.

Molly nods, hands it back to him.

"Is it strong enough?" P says.

"I guess."

"Wolf said it had a better chance of working if we made it real strong, but not crazy strong. Maybe I should have said more about how you would be hurt—I mean about what would happen to you if he didn't come up with the coin."

"Maybe."

"Yeah. Well I'll make it stronger the second time. He should get this tomorrow. That's the 22nd. The next night me and Wolf'll spell it out for him."

"What'll you say?" Molly says.

"What?"

"About what you'll do to me if he don't come up with the coin."

"Yeah. Well I'll say that we'll shoot you in the back of the head and dump you in a rad-fill."

"Big deal."

"I'll say we'll cut off your arms."

Molly smiles. "That all?"

"I'll say we'll cut off both arms and both titties and send him one of your small pink nipples to prove we mean it."

"Better," Molly says.

"Yeah, well it ain't all that easy coming up with this stuff. I'll talk with Wolf."

"Old Wolf."

"Right. Which means he'll take a nice cut too."

"So what?" Molly says.

"Right. If the old man gives us what we want we can take care of Wolf. Hey, where'd you get the coin to buy this shit, Mol?"

She don't answer.

"You said you wouldn't be into that shit again, Mol.

"Didn't do much," Molly says. "Hand-job."

"Bullshit. You couldn't buy this shit with what you got from a hand-job."

"You'd be surprised, cowboy. Some johns think I'm worth big coin."

P grins in spite of himself, puts his arm around her. "They're the smart ones."

He tries to kiss her but can't find her lips.

"This is some tasty shit," he says.

"It's getting good," Molly says.

"It's the belt," P says.

Molly and P go to the tower.

When ESSO became EXXON they erected a 97-floor tower with a huge gold-plated replica of the EXXON logo on top. One of the twelve freight elevators was usually left unattended, which is how they got to the top.

Some of the others were there: Magda, Dot, F, Loraine, Long M, Prince. They're all in with some tasty shit Wolf got for them. Long M's only fifteen but he's about six-eight, freaky. He hangs out with Sylvie, except Sylvie was sent to the Rack after her fourth OD. Long M gets off on sounds, just about never removes his headset.

43

Magda is sitting on top of the high railing facing the others. She's almost eighteen, been on her own for about five years. Has five sisters, all younger, and all her parents do is work. Which is what everybody else's parents do, except six kids in one family is crazy, especially girls. Magda probably makes bigger coin than both her parents together, only she has a big habit. Also she is good about keeping her friends in. Magda is only a little washed-out looking, blond, with a big chest. Johns dig her. She's been on the strip for a long time, has a whole lot of steadies.

The Tattoo Prince is off to the side by himself.

"Whatchoo got new?" P says.

Prince pulls up his shirt, pointing to behind his left shoulder: a long box, oblong-shaped, with the lid up and what looks like a head inside.

"Tasty," P says. "How the hell you get back there? Must be triple-jointed."

Prince grins.

To F, P says, "Where's Wolf at?"

F shrugs.

"You see Wolf?" P asks Magda.

Magda shakes her head. "Not since he laid this shit on. Want a jolt?"

P and Molly do. They do it away from the wind, using Molly's belt.

"Good. Real tasty," P says. "What's for tonight, Magda?"

Magda shrugs. "Spazzing."

"At the Inst?" Molly says.

"Sure," Magda says.

The Inst is the spazz-barn downtown. Live band usually. Lots of sound. Only a few of the kids still danced. Most everyone spazzed.

P mailed the letter to Molly's father, they hung out on the strip, dropped some blueys, then went to the Inst. One of the bike tribes was there bashing some guys. In the center of the floor while the others spazzed. When it was over—the

44

ass-kicking—one of the kids that worked there mopped up the blood and stuff. Bike tribes did this pretty regular and it was almost always over drugs.

Wolf was there but like always there were people around him. He saw P and made the "it's cool" sign with his fingers. P and Molly spazzed until the Inst closed at four. Then they went back to P's lid. Loraine and F were there, coupla others too. F squirted his name and Loraine's on the wall with blood. F was always squirting his blood around after he fixed. Molly and P were going to save their shit for the next day, but they ended up fixing right then and not getting to sleep. Next morning late P went to the strip to make some coin. P had a spazzy look about him and a sort of baby face and the homo johns dug him. Janes too. Molly didn't like the idea of him humping or even doing anything else with janes. Johns weren't that bad 'cause she knew P wasn't getting off on it.

Molly hung around the lid, watched the tube, slept some. Later she went out to West Artery thinking maybe she'd find that old man who paid her good for a hand-job. But she didn't see him and ended up doing a number with a coupla other johns.

Pretty much all the kids worked the strip, even Loraine who hated doing it. Molly and the others did it without getting into it, sort of separating themselves. But Loraine never got the hang of this, and after she did a few johns she was always blown out. Loraine was small and thin with long beautiful black hair like velvet, and her being scared and small turned the johns on. She had a lot of steadies.

Molly and Loraine got to the Inst at about eleven but only F, Loraine's old man, was there.

"Where's P?" Molly said.

F shrugged. "I saw him on South Artery early on. Busy night tonight. Some kind of war going on in the colonies. Johns were full of it."

"What do you mean?" Molly said.

"War," F said. "A small one from the sound of it. I didn't

know about it till one of the johns said it. I guess it's on the tube."

"Let's spazz," Loraine said, tugging at F's sleeve.

They went onto the floor. Molly went into the toilet and stuck some shit. Just a little, wasn't top-grade. She went out and spazzed with Long M. Long M kept his headset on real loud even with the live band blasting it.

"Where's P at?" Long M asked.

Molly shrugged.

Magda came in. She gave Molly three or four blueys with some cherry pop.

"Where's P?" Magda said.

"Don't know," Molly said.

"Johns are a little out of it tonight," Magda said.

"That's what F said. I didn't catch it. Something about a war."

Magda laughed. "Want a jolt?"

Molly shrugged. "I'll wait for P."

One of the bike tribes showed up and pretty soon they were smacking around some guys. They were using their chains so it got pretty messy. Then somehow Long M got into the action, like someone pushed him or something, so the bikers kicked his ass too. One of them tore Long M's earphones from his head and splattered the unit on the floor. When the fighting let up Magda and Molly dragged Long M to the side and patched him up a little. It looked like his nose was broke and coupla teeth were chipped. All he wanted was a jolt, which Magda gave him with her own kit.

P never made it to the Inst. Molly went back to the lid but he wasn't there, and some kid who was crashing there said that P hadn't been around. It was about an hour before light. Molly went out again, got a ride to South Artery which was where P and the others played rough for coin. From the looks of it that action was still going down. Whole lot of parked cars, johns inside. Other johns walking up and down the strip, some of them negotiating with the roughs. One john was going down on a rough right there, the rough leaning back on a railing. Molly asked Fritz, who was roughing, about P. Fritz said he was around someplace.

Molly walked for a while longer and then she saw him. P was getting out of a sportscar which had just pulled up. He didn't see Molly at first, but then he did.

He put his arms around her. "What are you doing here?"

"What happened to you?"

"Hey, this is big coin, girl. I already made enough to keep us in Wolf's best shit for three, four days."

Molly just looked at him. His eyes looked like he was dropping uppers. He looked beat.

"They made war again," P said. "In the Indian Ocean someplace from what they say. The johns are full of it because for them it means coin."

Molly didn't follow.

"Which means your old man," P said. "With the coin he stands to make from the war I can't see him griping about laying out a little for his only daughter."

"Let's go back to the lid," Molly said.

P had his arms around Molly's shoulders but he was looking past her.

"Not yet. Still too much coin here. Most action I ever saw here."

"What are you doing?" she said.

"Huh?"

"You letting them come in you?"

"No, huh-uh. Same like before. No humping. Don't matter to the johns neither. They just want to throw their coin away."

P waved to someone over Molly's shoulder.

"Look, Mol, you go back to the lid. I'll catch you there later. Tonight me and you and Wolf touch your father."

"Yeah, my father. You're more into that than into me."

"What do you mean? You're wrong, girl. This is special tonight. This coin's gonna get us the best in we ever got. And the coin from your father's gonna keep us in. That's how it's gonna be."

Molly backed away from him, turned, began to walk. But then decided she wouldn't go to the lid. It was light, the city was up. She bought a newspaper and looked through it for some mention of the scam. Too soon. Tomorrow it would be in the papers for sure. On the tube. The front page was all about this new war in the Indian Ocean. Molly tossed the newspaper on top of a parked car. She was thinking whether she really wanted to go through with the scam at all, whether she wanted to be *in in in* all the damn time. P got her pissed, spreading for the johns—she didn't believe he wasn't humping—spreading his damn ass for the johns.

She was needing a boost. She had walked past South Artery where the homos were. Past Rad-Fill C where the radiation waste was dumped. Couldn't be more than 6:30. Traffic already heavy both ways on the Artery. She wiggled her ass, stopped, took out her compact, put on lipstick. Someone honked his horn. Youngish john in a big car. She motioned with her head, he turned down a utility road. Molly walked up to the car and got in. He started the car with his left hand, his right hand gripped her thigh.

Molly pushed his hand away.

"What do you want?"

He grinned. "Guess."

"No humping," she said.

"Why the hell not?"

"No humping, that's it."

He shrugged. "Blow-job then."

"Cost you fifty."

He looked her over with one eye. "You must be pretty stuck on yourself."

She shrugged. "That's the price."

He reached across her and opened the door. Stopping the car he pushed her out.

"Your lips are too thin," he shouted at her.

"Lousy shit!" she shouted at him, the diesel from his car in her face.

Traffic was heavy—she had a hard time getting off the Artery to the pedestrian strip. A short while later another john, sort of old-looking, pulled over. Paid thirty for a hand-job, then dropped Molly at Magda's lid.

Magda was inside alone, laying on her bed watching the tube.

"I need a boost," Molly said. "I got coin."

"In the drawer," Magda pointed. "Take what you need."

Molly used Magda's kit, gave herself a heavy jolt. In fact she felt a little like she was going to OD. But it was okay. She got into the low wide bed with Magda and watched the tube. After a time she slept. When she woke the tube was still on and Magda was sleeping. Molly slept some more. When she awoke again Magda was standing naked, putting on her makeup. Molly had seen Magda naked before but had never noticed how tracked up her legs were, even her feet.

"How you feeling?" Magda said.

"Okay. Little dizzy."

Magda nodded.

"You gonna leave now?" Molly said.

"In a bit." Magda sat down on the bed. "Is it true what I heard?"

Molly looked at her.

"You and P gonna pull a scam?"

Molly nodded.

"Who came up with that? P?"

"P and Wolf," Molly said.

"Wolf? How'd he get a piece of this?"

Molly shrugged. "I guess P told him."

"Anything happen yet?" Magda said.

"What do you mean?"

"The scam start yet?"

"Yeah. P sent the kidnap letter to my father yesterday. Tonight him and Wolf are gonna phone my father, tell him where to leave the coin. Tell him some other stuff too."

"And Wolf is kinda helping P to keep the scam running slick, is that it?"

"I guess," Molly said.

"How much coin we talking about?"

"Eight hundred thousand."

Magda just looked at her.

"What's the matter?" Molly said. "Don't you think it'll work?"

Magda shrugged. "Gotta go." She touched Molly's hair and left.

Molly got up and drank some cherry pop from the fridge. Her stomach felt lousy. She went into the toilet in the hall but it wasn't any good, she was as clogged as ever. She smoked one of Magda's cigarettes, then brushed her teeth with Magda's toothbrush. She went outside and was surprised how late it looked. Lots of wind too.

She walked for a while, taking the utility roads away from the Artery. Turning a corner she saw a crow land on the broken-up pavement, scrape with its beak at a dead blackbird that was stuck to the ground, then fly away with the remains in its talons. Suddenly another small blackbird was pursuing the crow real close, badgering it so that the crow had to perch on a ledge still with the dead bird in its claws. The blackbird perched close to it screaming at it. After a bit the crow took off and so did the blackbird flying above and below the larger bird, still on its ass. Flew out of sight.

Molly was walking to P's lid, but the wind was getting to her. She turned up to the Artery and got a cab, but then when they got to P's lid she saw she had no coin, must've left it on Magda's table. The cab driver wouldn't trust her to go into P's lid and get some coin and instead honked his horn for about ten minutes until Wolf came out. Wolf gave the driver coin and Molly went in with him to P's lid. P was laying on the bed real fucked-up.

"That was a mistake you just made, Molly," Wolf said.

She looked at him.

"By tonight your picture will be on the tube and in the papers and you just led that cabby right to where you were gonna hole up."

"Oh, I didn't think of that. Anyways, I don't think I want to go through with it—the scam."

Wolf laughed. "Too late now, girl. We already phoned your father. The drop is scheduled for tomorrow dawn. I'll put you up in my place."

"What's up with P?" she said.

"P's about to make it to the moon. Want some shit?"

"I guess."

"Later," Wolf said. "At my place."

Wolf pulled P out of bed and they went outside into Wolf's car. Wolf lived near West Artery in a regular flat, two rooms and a bathroom inside. He laid P down on the bed. P was still looking bad, like he almost OD'd or something.

Wolf said, "P'll pull out of it. He took too large a jolt. This shit's tasty. Let me cook you a dose."

Molly fixed. Wolf was right, it was good. Wolf always came up with tasty shit. Meanwhile P was pulling out. Molly laid on the bed next to him and they held hands.

Wolf turned on the tube and after a while they saw Molly on the screen, as well as a copy of the scam letter P had sent. Her father also came on speaking about how much he wanted her back, that the kidnappers shouldn't harm her, that they would get their money. Then Molly's mother came on, looking bushed as usual, saying she loved her daughter. Then some high cop came on saying the police would abide by her father's wishes and not try to ambush the kidnappers. That was it.

Wolf went out.

Molly helped P undress and they screwed. Then they laid in bed smoking cigarettes and drinking cherry pop. They kept the tube on without sound till they saw her picture flash on the screen. It was pretty much a repeat of the first thing they saw except in this one Molly's father and mother were together. Her father had his arm around her mother's· shoulder. Molly felt her eyes fill—but then she giggled. So did P. It was the only time Molly had seen her parents touch since she was real small. In fact she didn't remember them touching then either, except she assumed they did. The same high cop came on saying the same things as before. Then another cop without a uniform said some things about how they would not interfere with the kidnapping so as to ensure Molly's not getting killed and stuff. They turned down the sound again.

Molly said, "I'd like us to get off shit for good."

"What do you mean?"

"With the scam money. Let's get off the shit and just go somewhere."

"Yeah," P said.

"Let's just go somewhere," Molly said. "Far away where we could like . . . be away from this."

"Yeah," P said. Then: "Eight hundred thou's a lot of coin. We'd never have to worry 'bout being low on shit."

"It ain't that great," Molly said. "Being in and stuff."

"Yeah, only what else is there? Who we gonna talk to?"

"What do you mean?" Molly said.

"We hardly know anybody who don't use. 'Cept Wolf."

"Yeah, Wolf," Molly said.

They lay on the bed and watched the tube.

"Where do you want to go?" P said.

"Huh?"

"When we get coin? Where do you want to go?"

"I don't know. Near the sea. I like water."

"The sea's fucked over," P said. "All those nuclear spills and shit."

"Not everywhere," Molly said. "It's not fucked over everywhere."

"I like mountains," P said.

"Right, we could go there. Mountains. Get a cabin."

P laughed.

"Why you laughing?"

"Ain't no more cabins," P said. "We'd have to get a condo. Which'd cost about what we're getting from the scam. Less what we give Wolf."

"How much we give Wolf?"

"Hundred fifty thou."

"That much?"

"Yeah."

"Whose idea was it in the first place?" Molly said. "Yours or Wolf's?"

"Kinda both. I guess his though."

"Magda was asking about it," Molly said. "The scam."

"Magda?"

"Yeah. I was with her when you were with the johns. Spreading for the johns." Molly pulled away from him. P touched her head with his hand. "Don't get pissed with me. I couldn't let that coin go."

"Why not? We're about to get eight hundred thou. Ain't that enough?"

"Ain't never enough," P said. "Besides, what if it don't work?"

"You mean my father backing down?"

"Right. Or setting us up."

"That's what Fritz said," Molly said. "Fritz said something about it maybe not working."

"That's what I mean. This was supposed to be between me and you and Wolf. And now Fritz and Magda and who knows who else knows all about it. We shoulda been cool."

"You're scared," Molly said. "Why don't we drop it? There's time. I'll just show up at my mother's and say I was let go. That the kidnappers got scared and let me go."

"Too late," P said. "It's too late to drop it."

"You know something?" Molly said. "I'm scared too. This is the first time I'm like really feeling it."

"The shit's wearing off," P said. "Let's fix."

"It's kinda soon," Molly said. "Why don't we just stick some? Small boost."

"Small boost won't do me," P said, getting up. "Where the hell's your belt? Damn! It must be in my lid. Which ain't too damn smart. Not if the cabby leads the cops there."

"Just a sec," Molly said. "Wolf put a whole lot of stuff from your lid on the floor over there."

She got up and went to the corner of the small room. She held up the belt.

"Wolf's cool," P said.

"Someone's got to be," Molly said.

P began to work on the shit.

"Not too much," Molly said. "You want to be clear for the scam."

"Scam ain't till dawn—six a.m."

"But you're gonna phone one more time, right? My father?"

"Wolf's doing it from the outside. Phoning at ten. No, ten-thirty. I'll be okay by morning."

"Who's picking up the coin?"

"Me. Deal is soon's I have the coin and am out of sight, Wolf signals you to go on to Getty at East and Seminole. Where your father'll be. You'll be waiting for the signal at East and Pugh."

"Then what?"

P was cooking the shit.

"Then we join up and spend the coin."

"What happens if my father . . . sends me away?"

"Like where?"

P had Molly's belt around his arm.

"Like nowhere," Molly said. She laid down on the bed on her stomach.

After he fixed P laid down next to her talking soft.

"We'll get together, Mol. Ain't no way we won't. Your old man makes the scam coin back in insurance. Plus he writes it off his taxes. He'll probably end up making more than he gave up. That's the way the shit works for the rich. How about a boost?"

"No."

"Little boost?"

"No—okay. Little."

Molly was going to just stick some, but she ended up using her belt for a fix.

"Guess what?" she said to P.

"What?"

"My birthday is Saturday. Just remembered."

"Hey," P said. "Sixteen, right?"

"Uh-huh."

"That's good. Your old man'll never let anything happen to you on your birthday."

"If he remembers."

"Did he last year?"

"I can't remember," Molly giggled.

She and P tried to screw but were too fucked-up. They smoked cigarettes, drank cherry pop and watched the tube. Every time the news came on there was something about the scam and Molly saw her face. It got to the point where it had nothing to do with her. Just a face of a thin girl with long brown hair. Daughter to an important-looking man with gray temples, and a wasted-looking woman who looked like the daughter but with wrinkles. There was also a lot of stuff on the new war in the Indian Ocean but Molly couldn't get what it was all about.

After a time she slept.

Someone was shaking the bed. Wolf, trying to get P up.

"Come on," Wolf said. "It's nearly ten. We have to phone the old man at quarter to eleven."

"I thought *you* were going to phone," Molly said.

"No," Wolf said. "P made the first contact, so it gotta be P."

"Where you phoning from?" Molly asked.

"Outside, couple of kilometers from here. Come on, P." Wolf shook him hard.

Finally P got up, Wolf got him dressed, and they left. Molly fell out again and for the first time in a long time she dreamed. She remembered it when Wolf and P came back in slamming the door. *She is on the Artery walking barefoot against the traffic. All the cars and trucks are white and moving in the other direction. And then she isn't walking but sliding on her feet, first sort of medium-speed, then fast, then out-of-control; the head-lights don't see her, the cars somehow don't hit her. This changes:*

she is in a black steep tunnel still between the speeding cars and trucks and she is rolling—hurtling—down-grade over the rough surface, her arms and legs bruised and bleeding, shredding loose from her body. While all the headlights in the white long cars are speeding the other way . . .

P stuck a lit cigarette in her lips.

"Done," he said.

"You phoned?"

"Right. He picked up on the first ring. No hassles. The coin'll be there at six. I even reminded him of your birthday."

"Yeah?"

"I said if you want Molly in one piece for her sweet-sixteenth don't fuck up."

"What he say?" Molly said.

"He said he'd play it straight." P looked at Wolf.

"If he drops the coin," Wolf said, "but the coin is marked, I know a party that'll pick it up and give us back two-thirds in unmarked. But I doubt it'll be marked."

"Yeah," P said.

Molly and P leave Wolf's lid at five-fifteen. (Wolf leaves later for Coolidge Tower from where he sees the entire transaction.) P leaves Molly at East Artery and Pugh, then goes to Getty at East and Seminole. Soon as P cops the coin and is away free Wolf signals Molly with a white towel and she goes on to Getty and her father. Any kind of foul-up and Wolf signals with a red towel, meaning Molly cuts out back to Wolf's lid. That's the deal.

Only what happens is P gets to the Getty drop on time and is ambushed, shot in the head and chest from close range with silencer .22s. This done, Wolf signals with his white towel and Molly goes on to Getty where she is snatched by the law. They take her to a lock-up downtown where her mother is waiting for her. Nothing passes between them. From the lock-up Molly is transported that

56

same morning to the Rack, the detoxification center on Muscle Island.

With his needles, ink and two small brushes the Tattoo Prince has completed yet another homemade. On the instep of his left foot: *a large animal with a single curved horn and heavy udders, its head bent as if trying to crop the grass.*

SALAMANDER

"The Salamandre berith wulle, of which is made cloth and gyrdles that may not brenne in the fyre."

William Caxton, 1481

"Look at them trees."

A short spare elderly black man, with a shaven crown and fresh-looking burns on his temples, Bubba, manacled, walks between the guards.

"Will you look at them trees," Bubba says.

"Well, what about them?" Guard West says.

"They're beautiful. Beautiful trees."

It's a long trek. West figures he'll play along.

"What's so damn beautiful about the trees, Bubba?"

"Why, everything. They're green, quiet, high. The sap flows to the furthest branches. Every smallest bit is fed so . . . quiet."

After another few hundred meters over the uneven terrain, Guard East says, "Quiet matters to you, don't it, old man?"

Guard West says, "It sure as hell must. On the inside 'bout all there is is clanging, screaming—"

"And that other thing," East says.

West looks at him. "Right. That other thing."

They've covered a lot of ground. The prison tower can be seen behind them. They've walked for most of the day and still the rotating stone tower is visible behind them.

East says to Bubba, "I bet you haven't done this kind of trekkin'—"

"I like it."

"Ain't tired?"

"Naw."

"Where you from, Bubba?"

"You mean . . ."

"Before the joint. Where were you born at?"

"Before the joint?" Bubba chuckles. He gently rubs the burn on his right temple.

West says, "I'm gonna take a leak."

They pause.

Guard East says to Bubba, "Any family?"

"What you mean?"

West, urinating, says to East, "It done messed up his memory."

East nods.

They are walking. Behind them the fading sun, the rotating tower.

West is thick: long muscular torso, short thick bowed legs. Mustache, assertive chin, orange-red hair. Mid-thirties. He says:

"What you think? How much longer?"

East shrugs. "Couldn't say. Good while, I'd say."

West: "How we ever get this detail?"

East guffaws. "Warden."

West nods. "You met the warden, didn't you Bubba?"

"Who?"

"The Warden. He was there, wasn't he? At the . . . end?"

East: "Hell, he ain't never missed a execution in thirty-odd years, from what I hear."

West yaps sardonically. "Well he sure as shit missed this one, didn't he?"

East grins. "I bet he's pissed."

West: "You think?"

East spits. "Warden done hates to look bad. This shit"— with his head he motions to Bubba—"makes him look bad."

Guard West has loaned Bubba his pocket knife and Bubba is whittling a chunk of wood with his manacled hands while he walks. Guards walk on either side. It is dark, moonless, the path has narrowed, West uses his light.

"Tell you what," West says. "Only thing don't bug me 'bout this detail's the pay."

"Double-time," East says.

"Damn straight. Double-time no matter we wake, sleep, or shit."

"Or eat," East says. "I'm damn hungry right now." To Bubba: "Hows about it, old man? Little chow?"

"Little chow and a little drink," West says.

"I don't know about the drink," East says.

"Why not? Just a damn little bit. Warden didn't tell us nothin' 'bout not givin' him no drink."

"That's true. He's just a old man."

"He sure as shit don't walk like no old man. Hey, Bubba, you hungry?"

"Right there looks good," East says. "Let's set down right there. I'll get the fire."

Using the flash, West examines East's hair for lice, then East examines West's hair, finds some, picks them out.

"Am I clean?" West says.

"Not yet," East says. "What you been up to?"

"Aint been up to shit. It's goddamn cootie city in that place," motioning with his head to the prison tower.

"Hey Bubba," East says. "You lucky you done got your head shaved," laughing.

East is tall and narrow, somber-looking. Two deep furrows run the width of his forehead. Fifty years old. He says: "How did it feel, Bubba?"

Squatting between the guards, Bubba, manacled, is whittling his chunk of wood, which is less a chunk now than an elongated curve or arc.

"I mean right there at the end. Strapped in. Them goddamn things on your head. What were you thinking?"

"If it was me," West says, "I wouldn't be doing no thinking. I'd be shitting a goddamn brick."

"From what I hear it never happened before," East says.

"Must've been in the motor," West says.

"Warden says the motor was fine. Just been maintenanced."

"Freak goddamn thing," West concludes. "How come we only brung that little amount of whiskey?"

"Who knew how long we'd be trekkin'?"

"How much longer we got?"

"Damned if I know."

"Hey, don't fuckin' shout at me. I just asked a goddamn question."

"Well, it's a dumb-ass question and besides I didn't shout at you. I didn't volunteer for this detail."

"Damn straight."

Silence. Except for the crackling fire and the sound of the knife whittling the wood.

"What the hell you whittlin'?"

"This?" Bubba brings the wood up in front of his eyes. "A tree."

"A tree!" West says. "What kind of goddamn tree is that all twisted to hell?"

"A tree in the wind," Bubba says. "A birch tree in a strong wind."

West shrugs. "Whatever you say, old man." Yawns. "Let's have the knife. I'm gonna bag."

"Me too," East says.

Bubba tosses West the knife.

SECOND DAY

Coffee. Breaking camp. First few thousand meters in silence. Bubba whittling. Behind them in the morning mist, the prison tower. Both guards wearing sunglasses against the early glare.

West: "Who's gonna meet us?"

East: "Where you mean?"

West: "At the . . . where we're going."

East: "Dunno. Nobody said."

West: "Ain't they expectin' us?"

East: "Must be. Warden didn't give you the papers?"

West: "Whose?"

East: "Bubba's."

West: "Hell no. I didn't see no papers."

Brief silence.

West: "Hey, Bubba, where your papers at?"

East: "How would he know?"

West removes his cap and scratches his head.

"I'll tell you what," East says. "Warden done messed up."

"Messed up?"

"That's right. I figure he still didn't get over the damn thing not working. And old Bubba here to tell the tale."

"You know something? That's how it was the other time—the Warden. The Commissioner was inspectin' the joint and that faggot was cut in the ass. Remember? Shithouse detail, one of 'em broke the bleach bottle, stabbed the punk right in the ass just when the Commissioner was inspectin'. Warden was on the rag for a month. Whole shithouse detail sent to the hole."

East: "What you saying?"

West: "That Warden done messed up. Like you said."

They had left the institution early Monday. It was getting on to Tuesday dusk and they still weren't there. Ground was drier, hardly any grass, broken stone. Dwarfed trees, evergreen. Blue cloudless sky spotted with pink. Sun fading. No birds.

"How far you think we gone?" West says.

"Couldn't say. Twenty kilometers?"

"Twenty! Feels more like thirty-five, forty."

"How could it be thirty-five, forty? We can still see the friggin' tower behind us."

"That's true too. Still, I'd say at least thirty. What you think, Bubba? How many kilometers we gone?"

"Gone? Don't feel all that far to me," Bubba says. He is still whittling. The block of wood now looks pretty much like a birch tree bending in the wind. It's even forked at the trunk the way birches sometimes are.

After a pause East says, "I'm gonna remove the cuffs."

West: "How come?"

East: "Why not? He's a old man, ain't he?"

East removes the manacles from Bubba's wrists and fastens them to his belt. He says, "What got you in the joint in the first place, Bubba? What got you sent up?"

"Homicide," West says. "He stuck a dude in some bar someplace."

East says, "How old are you now?"

"Old?" Bubba says. "Couldn't really tell you."

"He must be near to seventy," West says.

"Seventy!" East says. "He sure as shit don't walk like no seventy. Let's set under that overhang. I'm blown out."

West lights a cigarette. "How much chow we got left?"

"'Bout for tonight and tomorrow."

"That should do us."

"Damn well better."

"Wish we had some whiskey."

THIRD DAY

East wakes up pissed. West already up, making coffee, clanging around. Bubba finished his birch tree and is now whittling something else out of another chunk of wood.

"Gimme that knife back," West says.

"Why don't you let him have the knife?" East says.

"Mind your fucking business," West says. "My knife."

Silence.

"You're acting like a goddamn kid," East says.

"I'm goddamn tired of this shit," West says. "When the hell we gonna get there?"

"We should get there by tonight. The latest. How much money you think they gonna pay us to move a old colored man from one joint to another?"

"Is that what it is—where we takin' him—another joint?"

"I reckon. What else can it be?"

"How come they didn't let him stay where he was at?"

"Warden didn't want it. He takes it personal the old man

didn't die like he was suppose to. And now they can't kill him a second time. That's the law. So the Warden's movin' him to this low-security joint. Whole lotta old cons there from what I heard."

"What's it called, this place where we takin' him?"

"Salamander," East says. "Salamander. Like the animal."

West gave Bubba the knife again. At midday they stopped at a creek to drink and bathe. It was hotter than hell and this was the first watering hole they saw so they took advantage. West and East stripped to their drawers and waded into the creek, while Bubba sat on the bank whittling. Later the three of them sat or lay on the bank.

West: "Bubba, you 'bout the only person I ever seen got that close to death and then didn't die."

East: "I had a uncle that happened to. He died of a heart attack—I mean his heart stopped. But then they brung him back."

"Was he different?"

"Yeah, he was. For a while he was a more quiet kind of person. Real quiet and calm. But then he became a prick again." East laughed. "When he died for real he was about as big a prick as he ever been."

"Bubba ain't no prick."

"Hell no. Bubba's a nice colored man. But then he coulda always been like this. I didn't know him before. You?"

"Naw. I seen him around. At chow, in the yard. That's about it. Bubba, did you change at all since you was electrocuted?"

Bubba scratched his temple with the knife blade. "You want to know how I was before? I was a mean son of a bitch."

West grins. "Yeah?"

"Shit, if this was before. Me with a knife, you two in your drawers—I woulda cut your white balls off and thrown them in the crik. Then I woulda used the knife to carve a little message on your stomach. On yours," Bubba motions to

West, "I woulda carved WHITE SCUM. On yours," meaning East, "I woulda carved WHITE PLAGUE."

Bubba didn't say this. He didn't say anything to West's question. Just made a small gesture with his head to acknowledge that he heard—and kept on whittling.

"What you whittlin' now?" West says.

"Now? Another tree."

"You sure do like trees," East says.

"Well, the other was a birch. This here gonna be a spruce."

"Spruce?"

"Yeah. Spruce a lot harder than birch. To whittle."

"How's that?" East says, head back, eyes closed in the sun.

"Well, a spruce is a cone tree, so that if you do it right you gonna have to get some cones in. Whittlin' cones ain't easy."

After lazing in the sun, they had to ford the creek, which Bubba did by stepping lightly from stone to stone. Neither of the guards could do this and both were sopping when they got to the other bank.

Moving again, guards walking more or less abreast, Bubba slightly behind to the left.

East: "What time you got?"

West: "Goddamn watch stopped. Musta gotten wet in the crik. Judgin' by the sun I'd say past three."

East, turning: "How come we can still see the tower?"

West, turning: "Damned if I know. It ain't as if we're on the plain. We been going up and down hills and we musta covered forty kilometers easy. But there it is, the goddamn tower. Don't even look that far away neither."

FOURTH DAY

Last of the coffee. Just one can of Spam, one can of beans. No smokes. No whiskey. They break camp in silence. West violently scratching his legs as he moves.

"Goddamn lice!"

"Don't kill 'em all," East says. "We may have to eat 'em 'fore long."

"Goddamnest fucking thing! Could we a went wrong?"

"What you mean?" East says.

"What in hell you think I mean? Gone wrong to this cunting place we going. This Salamander."

"But one way to go," East says. "We on it."

Silence.

"Tell you what," West says, glancing back at Bubba three or four paces behind. "I ain't got nothin' particular 'gainst this old man, but I wish to goddamn hell he died when he was suppose to."

East nods.

"If he done died like he suppose to," West says, "there'd just be another dead nigger con and that'd be the end of it."

"Well it didn't happen that way."

"What you sayin'?"

"I'm saying he *didn't* die like he was suppose to. He's right the hell there walkin' behind us, whittlin'—"

"Don't you think I see him?"

"Well! What you want?"

"I want to know what the hell is going on. Four goddamn days on the goddamn trail and look at that!" He turns and points. "Goddamn tower."

"You know what?" East says. "We give it one more day and if we don't get there we turn the hell back."

"What we do about chow? 'Bout smokes?"

"We gonna have to do without smokes. Gonna have to shoot us some birds or rabbits for chow."

"Shoot?"

"That's right. You a huntin' man."

"I don't think I seen a animal the whole time we been trekkin'."

"Me either. But that's because we weren't lookin' for 'em. I mean we in nature, ain't we? Gotta be animals."

Silence.

"I guess it's nature, like you say," West says. "But 'bout all there is is sand and rock. And sun. Feel that bitchin' sun, would you! What happened to the goddamn trees?"

"Damned if I know. I never been this direction before. Rabbits like this kinda terrain, though. Game birds too. We just gotta keep our eyes open."

West motions with his head: "Hey, Bubba."

Bubba keeps walking, whittling.

"Hey, coon. I'm talkin' at you. Keep your eyes open for rabbit and bird. Else we gonna have to shoot up your old black ass and eat *you*."

They stop after dusk to finish the last of their provisions. None of them has seen a bird or rabbit or anything else. The guards silently share the last of the Spam and the beans. Bubba squats on the other side of the fire whittling.

"Stop that goddamn whittlin'," West says. "I can't stand the noise. Gimme the knife back anyways."

Bubba makes a few more whittling cuts then tosses the knife on the ground near West.

"You know what?" West says. "I think we oughta cuff the nigger."

"What the hell for?"

"First of all, I don't believe he's no seventy years old. He couldn't be trekkin' and fordin' the crik like he does at seventy years old. And then I don't trust the son of a bitch. Not on a trek that's takin' us this goddamn long. I say we cuff him."

"Can't do it," East says.

"What you mean?"

"I left the damn cuffs back there someplace. I think by the crik."

"How in hell you do that?"

"I did it. What can I tell you?"

FIFTH DAY

Dawn, Bubba squatting on his haunches and whistling softly while the guards sleep. After a time they stir, sluggishly rise . . .

West: "I don't know what you want to do. And I don't give a good goddamn in hell neither. I'm turnin' back."

East: "Me too. At least all we gotta do is keep our eyes on that damn tower and move in a straight line. We do that we could maybe get to the crik by day after tomorrow. Maybe catch us some fish."

"Damn straight. We shoulda turned back yesterday. Or even the day before."

"Shit," East says. "We shouldna accepted this goddamn detail in the first place."

They are walking heavily in the direction of the prison tower: West, East behind him, Bubba behind East.

"What do we tell the Warden?" West says.

"Tell him to take a piss in the bitchin' desert. What in the hell can we tell him?"

"He's gonna be pissed."

"Fuck him. Better him pissed than me dead."

"Damn straight."

Trudging without talk.

"But you're right," East says. "He's gonna be pissed. He ain't gonna accept that we couldn't find this goddamn place. Salamander."

"No way."

"Huh?"

"I said if we come back with the old coon the Warden ain't gonna accept nothin'. Hey, Bubba," West says. "See what you caused us. Why the fuck didn't you just die in the fucking chair like every other sumbitch that was electrocuted?"

"What you think he'll do?" East says.

"Who's that?"

"Warden."

"Give us hell. If we're lucky. Bust us is what he'll probably do. Put us on roadgang detail."

"Or shithouse detail."

"Right," West says. "Make us make the faggots keep their dicks in their own pants. Wouldn't that be a bitch!"

Trudging in silence.

West moves closer to East, whispers, "I got a idea. Why don't we kill the nigger, then tell the warden he done died on us?"

"I hear you," East says.

"Shit. Even Warden wouldn't expect us to carry a old nigger killer's body back to prove he done died like we said he did."

"We could tell Warden the old man had a fit. Or choked on his food—"

"Don't say that word," West says. "Don't say nothin' 'bout no eatin', drinkin', or smokin' till we be doin' all three."

West withdraws his pistol from his holster and turns around. East does the same. Bubba the prisoner is gone.

After looking for the prisoner with drawn guns—not finding him—the guards sit on a rock.

"Told you we shoulda cuffed him."

"He won't get far," East says. "He don't have chow or water—"

"All he needs is a goddamn stone. We gotta sleep, don't we? Nigger'll kill us to hell in our sleep if we let him."

"We won't let him. One of us watch while the other sleep. Once he sees he can't get to us he'll give it up. If he don't we'll shoot him to hell. Either way we tell Warden he done died on us. Like you said."

The guards, pistols drawn, moving wearily in the direction of the rotating tower. They push ahead until they can't move another step, collapse on the dry pitted ground, sleep.

SIXTH DAY

When they wake the sun is high and their pistols are

gone.

"Coon!" West says.

"Gotta be."

"What in hell we do now?"

"What can we do? Keep pushin' till we get the hell back. If he'd a wanted to kill us he woulda did it when he took the guns, right?"

"Not if he wants to see us squirm first. Hey, did he rip off our water?"

East checks. "No. Water's still there. How the hell's he hangin' on without water's what I'd like—"

"How much we got?"

"Third of a canteen. Maybe a little less. Oughta keep us till we hit the crik. What about the knife?"

"Gone," West says. "He took the goddamn knife."

"Let's move it," East says.

For the first time since they started out six days before they spot animals: two ground squirrels, several rabbits, three or four quail. Weary, without weapons, without trees from which they could construct a bow or a sling, they're helpless. Again West lights into East for not having cuffed the nigger. East shouts back and soon they're grappling, rolling on the hot hard ground. This doesn't last; they roll away from each other and lie sprawled, exhausted . . .

East gets up first. "Sun's high. Better move."

At dusk they see two quail ahead of them on the trail, but by the time they pick up stones the quail have scampered and flown. Later they throw stones at a rabbit and a crow—no luck. They stumble on cussing Bubba, the Warden, each other. Especially Bubba. They fall asleep soon after dusk and don't awake until the following dawn.

SEVENTH DAY

They haven't gone more than a few hundred meters in the direction of the rotating stone tower when West reaches for the canteen which East is carrying.

East: "What you want?"

West: "Drink."

"Not now. We got too far to go to the crik."

"Now!" West tugs at the canteen. The stopper comes undone and the small amount of water remaining spills on the ground. West tilts the canteen into his throat, then falls on the ground and sucks at the spilled water. East kicks West in the side. West picks up a stone and smashes East below the knee, knocking him down. Then with the same stone he hits him in the face, on the head. Hits him on the head several more blows, with each blow falling exhausted onto East's body. Finally West gets up and struggles forward . . .

West did finally reach the creek, but only to stumble in the water and drown, his orange hair bobbing like algae on the creek's bottom. Or maybe he didn't drown, but drank and rested and made it back to the prison, where the Warden gave him hell and transferred him to roadgang detail.

Bubba? He made it easy to Salamander (the salamander gives me light and the power to see the second night). He's there now, with the others who passed through. They're old and colored and small in number. Bubba's with them in Salamander even as you are turning this page.

SHEEP

"Embrace the butcher"
Brecht

"I wouldn't have minded the Angels. I wouldn't have minded the Chosen Few. See, I always let her know she has a home wherever I am, in a bus or whatever. I said to her: 'Ronnie, I'll always call you and give you the longitude—like, you know, this is where I am at right now, and you have a home with me.' "

Who said that?

Ronnie's mom said that. I'll tell you about her in a bit. First I want to say that I have a surprise for you. I'm holding it in one hand behind my back. It's real, real American and it's state-of-the-art. Absolutely now. I'll give you a hint—it's one of the following: Environmental Cancer, The Information Explosion, Lifestyle, The Serial Murderer. Can you guess which one it is?

Lifestyle?

No.

Environmental Cancer?

Huh-uh. Guess again.

The Serial Murderer?

That's right. Absolutely. How did you guess?

(She shrugs)

Well, he's here in my left hand. His name is Rick and he has silky, light brown hair parted on the left side, and nice small ears close to his head. Go ahead, pet his ears—but be careful of his teeth, they're small and white but real sharp, and once they grip you they tear and tear.

Why?

Because he don't know how to be just friends, that's why. And he never learned to respect another's personal space. Because of the breakdown of the nuclear family and TV. TV puts everything at the same level, right?

(She shrugs)

Well, it does. Besides, everybody white has a car and in your American car on your great American freeways you can drive and drive. It's true we don't have a frontier anymore, but we're bigger than heck. And you know what it's like? It's like turning on the TV and eating your breakfast cereal. That's what Rick the serial murderer did. Yeah, Rick, like who I have in my hand. In his '82 metallic-red TransAm with the gold racing stripe he averaged a hundred and sixty thousand miles a year driving west to east, north to south.

Why?

Oh, looking for girls. To bite them and rape them and kill them. To lure them into his TransAm, and there's a whole lot of ways of doing that. If Rick's white smile and small ears and typical-boy-next-door spiel don't do it, he'll snap on his false leg-cast and ask this pretty young miss to help him to his TransAm which once he gets her near his TransAm—

forget it. That's what happened to Ronnie. And that was Ronnie's mom (a blue-collar gal, real hung-up on bikers, has "Harley Davidson" tattooed on her left shoulder, and the personalized license plate on her '79 Pinto says "Wyld Fire"). Ronnie's mom lamenting and stuff, saying she wished Ronnie had been kidnapped by the Hell's Angels because the Angels are good outlaws, whereas Rick, he raped and bit and killed her—Ronnie.

Is he real strong?

Rick? Heck yeah. Rick's an all-around athlete. At Alamo High down there in Texas he lettered in baseball, football and track. Also two years in a row he won the Punt, Pass and Kick competition for ten and eleven year-olds for all of south-central Texas. He grew up in San Antone, you know, which is why he has this real neat way of saying things. His mom and dad divorced real early and so his mom was always out of the house doing her secretarial work. That's what I mean about the breakdown of your nuclear family. Do you have any idea what the divorce rate is in America? Young Rick was left to his own devices. But he didn't really start doing his thing—I mean serial murder—till after he graduated from Alamo High, 189th in a class of 303, but one of the best athletes like I said and voted MOST TELE-GENIC—they had their own TV hookup and stuff at Alamo.

(Pause)

You know what serial murder is, don't you?

Ye-es.

What is it?

Well, it's like murdering . . . killing a whole lot of people—girls and stuff.

75

No, huh-uh. You're thinking of your mass murderer, YY dummies like Speck and Whitman and Unruh, as well as a lot of inner-city folks, go off the deep end one hot summer day all worked up and shit. Your serial murderer ain't that. Does little Rick here, with his sandy smooth hair and small nice ears and straight slender shoulders look like a YY dummy? You want to pet him again?

(She nods)

Go ahead. Pet his ears. You can pet his nice flat tummy too. But be careful of those teeth. 'Cause that powerful TransAm car of his is real close by, and once he gets you in there, with his cassette deck and stuff, plus what he keeps under the back seat. See, your serial guy is calculated. Rather than kill eight at once, he'll kill you eighty over eighteen months. You see what I'm getting at? And he won't blow you away with a large-caliber, but will use his own hands, snap your neck, throttle, whatever. He's real persuasive.

How come?

Well, persuasive sells. And the right kind of sell will get you into all kinds of sweet tight spots. That's why serial murder is hot now. The FBI says that out of a total of fourteen thousand homicides committed last year in the continental United States, 8.7 percent were "stranger-to-stranger" murders. And you know why? Because the nuclear family has been fractured and you can't even tell real from Xerox anymore.

Oh! He snapped at me with his teeth.

Sorry about that. I almost forgot about those teeth of his, they're so pretty. Do you know what the old judge said to Rick when he sentenced him down there in west Florida?

Rick had been down there doing his thing on some college gals, bagged half-a-dozen of 'em before they nailed him. Anyway, with an air-tight case against him, the suspected murderer of maybe forty-eight young gals, mom's daughters—this crusty old judge fell lock, stock and barrel for Rick's sell. Just before sentencing him he said: "You're a clean-cut young man, and I like you. If things were a little different I would have liked to see you trying a case in my court instead of being tried like you are. Good luck to you, partner. And Godspeed."

Why did he say Godspeed?

Just a way of speaking. It wasn't like he was sentencing Rick to the Chair, you understand. Rick got himself a couple of life sentences, but simultaneous, which means that he's eligible for parole in about fifteen.

He'll be out again in fifteen years?

Well he's pretty and Christian and white, ain't he? He'll be out in fifteen easy. Yeah, chances are he killed and raped forty or fifty gals in the three-year period from when he left San Antone in his metallic-red TransAm for Oceanside California to visit a buddy. Seems he picked himself up a female hitchhiker on I-15 going west into California. He did a number on her, I can tell you—teeth, rape, throttle, the whole bit. And it seemed to like whet his appetite because he never did stop off at his buddy's. Instead he kept moving north up to Washington state, then east and south, sometimes hanging out in a place, working part-time, raping and killing gals just about wherever he went.

What did he work at?

You name it. Like I said before, he was real telegenic, so he worked as a model on TV and stuff, big bucks for diddly.

Hey, do you recognize him from TV? Let me squeeze the back of his neck to make him grin. He did your lite beer and underarm deodorant and Dr. Pepper, lots of stuff. Anyway, he moved around getting himself young gals—that's how he liked them, about your age. Did his shit and dumped them, never took their money. Which is another thing: your serial killer don't do it for coin. But the thing is the prosecutor could only pin two homicides on him for sure, which is the reason for the simultaneous life sentences rather than successive and no chance of parole.

Why did the judge call him partner?

Shoot. You got to remember that your American judge is used to sentencing blacks and Chicanos or white YY dummies with homemade tattoos on their knuckles. Rick with his sandy smooth hair and small ears close to his head was like a breath of Spring to the judge. And like I said, Rick knows how to sell: he didn't come on mental or nothin'. He came on preppy, real slender. Had the old judge in his hip pocket.

(Pause)

You want to work his joy stick? No problem . . . Does that feel nice?

Uh-huh.

That's another thing about your serial murderer, and I've been saving it for now on purpose. He's not like your modern-day political assassin: Oswald, Sirhan Sirhan, Bremer— all screwed up between the legs. Like Oswald was supposed to have said: "My penis made me do it." Well, your serial murderer don't have any problems with that stuff. Bundy, Wilder, the Boston Strangler guy, even John Wayne Gacy. They could do it. Fact is they could maybe do it too good. Or too weird anyhow. Yeah, Rick, he was on the sadistic side, he liked to bite while he scored. And I mean bite. Some of the gals had bite-sized marks all over the place, and some actually had flesh-chunks like excised, missing. Weird stuff, but not all that different from what you see on TV, in store windows, magazines. Am I right?

(Pause)

I don't know.

Well get your fingers away from Rick's joystick and switch on your brain. I'm only joking. You're a young person, you've never even known the nuclear family unit. Your mom works outside the home, don't she?

(She nods)

What does she do? Secretary?

Real Estate.

Ah. You see. Your dad and mom are divorced?

(She nods)

All right, let's try something, okay? Watch Rick's lips and teeth and forget about my hand at the back of his neck. Just answer him the way you would in real life, okay?

* * * * * *

Rick (stopping his TransAm between the evangelical church and the shopping plaza): Wanna rad?
Girl (pausing): You talk funny.
Rick (laughs): I'm from San Antone. My name's Rick. I bet

79

you've seen my face.

Girl: Yeah? Where at?

Rick: TV. I do Dr. Pepper. Also Lite Beer.

Girl: So you're rich, right?

Rick: You wanna find out? Stick your hand in my pocket. This one. Anything you find in there you keep.

Girl (looks briefly down at his pocket, then starts to walk again): I don't believe you've got anything in your pocket.

Rick (starting his TransAm, purring alongside the walking girl): Best way to test your unbelief is to take a chance.

Girl: Yeah! What does that mean?

Rick: How old are you? I bet you're not a day older than fourteen.

Girl: I'm sixteen.

Rick: Yeah? You're real cute. You ever do any modeling? Like on TV?

Girl (stops again): No.

Rick: (stops his TransAm): Well, we sure could use a young cute gal with long brown hair and a nice figure—

Girl: How do *you* know?

Rick: What?

Girl: That I've got a nice figure?

Rick (grins): I could tell. I watched you from the time you went into Runner's World and bought that cute pair of nylon running shorts. Kelly green, right? I watched you try them on too—

Girl (starts to walk again): You're weird, you know that?

Rick (starting his TransAm, driving alongside her): You run, right? Jog?

Girl: Who wants to know?

Rick: Hey, this is bullshit. (Jumps out of his TransAm, grabs hold of the girl's neck from behind, drags her into his TransAm.)

* * * * * *

That didn't work all that good. You weren't concentrating.

(She shrugs) *Where's he at now?*

Rick? Rick's in State Prison down there in west Florida. He's a consultant for the made-for-TV-movie they're doing on his life. They're paying him in the high six figures. I reckon they must be about finished shooting by now. Keith Carradine plays Rick. Do you like him—Keith Carradine?

He's old.

(Laughs) Not really. Comes from a well-known acting family. Actually, his father was the only one that could act. John Carradine. He wanted to do serious stuff for the stage but ended up doing mostly horror flicks in Hollywood. He had a gaunt ominous look about him, and a rich fine voice. Keith Carradine lacks voice but has the look: tragic and supple and well-groomed. Plus he has a head full of white small teeth. Just like Rick. I bet you'd like to see the movie, right? The made-for-TV-movie on Rick's life?

When is it?

In the Fall. Next Fall, right before the elections. When all the new shows come on. When folks figure to be glued to the tube.

(Pause)

You want to press any more of Rick's buttons?

(She shakes her head no)

Okay, I'm going to put him back in my Samsonite attaché case. Then I'll take you to Pizza Hut.

Wendy's.

All right. Wendy's. We'll get you something to eat. You look like your attention has waned some and an ice-cold styrofoam cup of Dr. Pepper'll perk you back up. Then I want to show you something you'll like a lot.

What?

You want me to show it to you now?

(She shrugs)

Well, since it don't matter to you, I'll wait till after you've had your burger and fries and Dr. Pepper at Wendy's. I'll just tell you that it's real American, what I've got, and state-of-the-art. New, now, new. Absolutely.

Can I put it in my mouth?

Yes you can.

Can I wrap my petal-like legs around it?

Uh, yes you can.

And it's not boring?

No, no. Heck no.

(Pause)

I don't believe you.

On the way to Wendy's we had to pass the railroad station. Except for elderly widows with cataracts, and the handicapped, folks drove their cars or flew, so when I saw a long line of boxcars stalled at the station, I knew it was something else. Actually I smelled it first, then, pulling the girl by the hand, I looked into one of the boxcars and saw sheep: gaunt in their fleece and excrement, downcast eyes, one with a withered almost-born lamb protruding from her haunch, those that could still stir scratching at each other's fleece for food. I moved to another car and it was the same— dead and near-dead sheep, obviously a long time on the rails and unfed, massed almost on top of each other, en route to the slaughterhouse somewhere, and the amazing thing was how silent they were, not even a baa.

TWO

JOHN CROW

"I am not where I think, and I think
where I am not."

Jacques Lacan

PRELIMINARY

With its short legs, long trunk and pointed muzzle, it resembled a miniature dachshund. It crossed the pocked road,
slid beneath the high fence of the rented villa in coastal Jah,
and sidled up to the wife and husband tourists having their
Planter's Punch on the veranda. They fed it and tentatively
stroked it and the animal returned each of the next four days
at approximately the same time.

By the fifth day, as the tourists were preparing to return to
their own country, the animal had won them over completely. Previously it had come just before dinner; if it happened to return *now*, in mid-morning, that would be *kismet*;
the tourists would attempt to smuggle the animal back to
their own country.

It came, the tourists stroked it, fed it, and smuggled it into
their country. The night after they returned, while they
slept, the creature attacked them, then made off somehow
into the black city streets. It had been rabid: the husband
died; the wife recovered only after the painful, extensive
treatment.

What had resembled a dachshund was, the American
medical examiner concluded, a Jahian rat.

VITAL

4207 square miles, at 19 degrees north, 78 west: we are in Jah in the northern Caribbean, the largest English-speaking country of the *West Indies*. Correction: *Commonwealth Caribbean*; this, we are informed, is the designation the English-speaking former colonies prefer.

Jah's recorded history: Circa A.D. 750, "a cinnamon-hued aboriginal people" from the Orinoco headwaters in southeastern Venezuela commenced to arrive in their bamboo and reed canoes. These aboriginals established a culture of fishing, hunting, elementary farming, ritual games, barter . . . Transformed utterly at the tail-end of the 15th century, when the Spaniards landed with their crosses and crossbows and edicts and gold-lust and fierce pride.

By the time the British routed the Spaniards and wrested Jah in the mid-16th century, the aboriginals had been exterminated and the menial labor was performed by an estimated 200,000 African slaves.

Note: While the caucasians scrimmaged, some 20,000 slaves managed to escape into the sierras where, known as the John Crows, they would wage guerrilla war on the British colonists for nearly three centuries. These freedom-fighters appropriated the name John Crow ironically, since like the later and possibly derivative Jim Crow of the U.S., it signified a beaten, shuffling Negro:

> My name Jim Crow
> Wheel about and turn
> about, and do jus' so.*

Finally, in the early part of our own century, after innumerable costly skirmishes, the British tendered a peace offering, then underwrote the resettlement of nearly 12,000 John Crows in Liberia, West Africa. The fifteen-odd thousand who refused resettlement pledged themselves to the "Africanization" of Jah.

FAUNA

The European brown rat arrived in Jah on the ships of the Spanish conquerors. Two hundred years later the provident British introduced the ferret (*Mutela furo*) to combat the brown rat, but instead the ferret was overcome by the native chiggers. In 1883 the persistent British introduced the mongoose from Raj India where it had performed capitally against the Punjabi gray rat.

By this time the composition of the principal fauna had stabilized. In place of the liquidated aboriginals was a work force of 1.7 million chattel blacks from throughout Africa, with the largest numbers from the Gold Coast and southern Nigeria. Ibo, Ashanti, Yoruba, Bantu, Mandingo, Bongo, Concha, Congo, Nanga. Africans from warring tribes who spoke different dialects were routinely bound to the same plantation laird. An Irish planter saw it this way in 1838:

> The Bongoes, the Mandingoes, the Eboes, the Congoes, &c., &c., formed into exclusive groups, and each strove to be loudest in the music and songs, or rather yells, peculiar to their country; and their dance, if dance I must call it, was a display of unseemly gestures.*

Only fifteen years after its introduction it was estimated that the mongoose was saving Jah 120,000 pounds per annum. However, the brown rats that managed to escape became arboreal, and within half a dozen rat generations were as abundant as the smooth-billed ani (*Crotophaga ani*), national bird of Jah.

Moreover, the mongoose that had so distinguished itself in northwestern India virtually eradicated the Jah red iguana, which had been essential in controlling the malarial coastal mosquito.

AUTHOR

A.D. 1984. Does it matter that Q is here in magical, penurious Jah for "personal reasons"? August will mark the 20th anniversary of Jah's independence from the British. Q is sitting in the battered, crowded bus skimming a month-old copy of NEWSWEEK:

> The Soviet Union has established a category of mental illness for dissidents called "sluggish schizophrenia," which means a lengthy "institutionalization" for those guilty of "delusions of reformism."

The teeming bus, blazing sun; on the radio, very loud, the West African-accented music—called Puku—with its exuberant insurrectionist lyrics. Passengers swaying or tapping, dripping sweat. Patois banter, laughs. The bruised British Leyland bus skimming the narrow road. To the west: congenial azure sea. To the east: dense tropical bush. Beyond: the green wooded foothills of the New Abyssinia Mountains.

When Q asks the fellow on his left whether the bus will stop at Lambeth he says: "Yah mon."

The British parceled the country into counties: Cornwall, Middlesex, and Surrey; and the counties into parishes: Lambeth, Westmoreland, Trelawny, Clarendon, Manchester, Westminster . . .

From Lambeth Q makes for spirited coastal Patu, where it is market day. In Patu Q sees this decal on the seat of a young Jah woman's skirt: BLOOD, PEOPLE, LAND. He sees "John Crow" scrawled on several buildings, chalked on the street, once on a button on a very old man's cap.

Today is Q's birthday, he is freshly middle-aged.

From Patu Q changes busses for Dasheen, seven miles of white sand and tropical woodland on the Caribbean. Jah men and women come to Dasheen from throughout the island to sell trinkets and fruit and beer and the potent native cannabis to tourists. The sellers are referred to as "higglers." It is in Dasheen that Q hopes to meet with Cudjoe, Information Minister of the John Crows.

GEOPOLITICAL

A disease first observed among the earliest slaves that the Spanish wrested from Angola, but which has fulminated periodically among the other African groups now in Jah, is geophagy, or dirt-eating.

"The negroes are subject to a strange craving of the stomach for earth: earth-eaters are common upon almost every plantation. Many negroes consider a *mud-cake* as preferable to any other viand" (Stewart, 1808).*

PEOPLE

Gretchen, a tourist, complained to Q that when she and her roommate tried to shop in the small native market in Dasheen, the broad-hipped native matrons intentionally collided with them in the aisles. And the products themselves were "putrid": rancid tubs of butter, rusted tins of fruit . . .

The Kish in particular are scary, Gretchen says.

Kish is the Ethiopian-worshipping religious-political sect which includes, according to a recent estimate, 26 percent of the men and 11 percent of the women. Most of the Kish males wear dreadlocks, are strict vegetarians, and endorse the Africanization of Jah, which they mean to bring about through "active non-violence," after the examples of Gandhi, Martin Luther King, and especially Steve Biko. At the same time many Kish are said to be sympathetic to the violent John Crows.

The Kish Q has seen are physically impressive, with pliantly muscular bodies and intense high-boned faces. Their single unprepossessing feature is the eyes—the whites have become muddied from prodigious smoking of cannabis. The young women—whether Kish or not is not distinguishable—are graceful, high-breasted, at once languid and vibrant. From their mid-twenties the poorer Jah women (most) tend to gain weight, fade about the eyes.

Settling down on the sand next to middle-aged Q, the wide strawbasket still on her head, a higgler wants to sell. She has mangoes and paw paw and sweet sop and naseberries and Guinness beer and fresh aloe for sunburn. Her name is Mavis, she is about 16, with a radiant smile and a distended stomach—her navel protrudes like a small grenade beneath her shift. To Q she talks in standard English, to the Jahians who amble by she talks in Patois. Q buys a bottle of Guinness (brewed in Jah) and a strip of aloe for his pink burning skin.

FLORA, ETC.
From one of Columbus' party, 1494: "Silhouetted against the evening sky, arose sheer and darkly green Jah. The fairest island that eyes have beheld: mountainous and the land seems to touch the sky; very large, bigger than Sicily, and all full of valleys and plains, with a rich and fat soyle."*

This way still: the murdered blacks and aboriginals having fatted the soil. The hundreds of misery belts and shanty towns throughout the island? Another vitality against the tropical lush.

Impediments: Since the principal industries are tourism and bauxite mining, we see the erection of grand hotels with its correlate, piecemeal destruction of the shoreline. And we see and smell in Middlesex county the grandscale moonscaping of the land, the production of aluminum out of bauxite with American technology for U.S. consumption.

Blue mahoe, bamboo, mahogany, ironwood, silk cotton, mosquito wood, Carib Pine, breadfruit, pimento, satinwood, ackee, cashew, lignum vitae, ebony, red birch, nine species of mango, fifty-three species of palm, seventy-eight species of epiphyte (excluding the orchid). Epiphytes on every electrical wire, it seems: fragile, voracious little nests, feeding—thriving—on what's not visible.

PATOIS

"Hit no cum fuh we—de rebolution."

"Widout Lawd Jah folk dem nubba prasper."

"De boss Crow im white, lickle tings dem afeard a de big boss Crow."

"De mon im howe me money gone a Cuba."

"I'm walk strong, I'm lub sweet, I'm sleep hebby."*

"Don cuss alligator long snout till you cross riber done."*

AUTHOR

Errol, a Kish, will, he says, put Q in contact with Brother Cudjoe of the John Crows. Q is in Errol's open shed on the Dasheen beach. Errol is shaving a coconut with his machete. Another Kish is also in the shed, squatting, with a spliff in his mouth, scrutinizing his face in a broken hand-mirror.

Errol passes Q the coconut. After Q drinks the sweet water he returns the coconut to Errol who slices it in half with one deft machete stroke, fashions a "spoon" out of the rind and gives the halves back to Q.

"It put," Errol grins, "de sperm in your back."

Q eats the jelly with the spoon, then tosses the coconut onto a large pile. He hands Errol a two pound note.

Errol: "So you tink nice dis land of we, my bredda?"

Q: "I do. I'm disturbed, though, by the poverty, the hundreds of men like yourself I see everyday with no work."

Errol: "You say true, bredda. You say true."

Q: "What can be done, then?"

Errol: "I tells you what can be done, my bredda. I tells you a story of a mon im went so far out im not could cum bock . . . "

First Errol takes the spliff from the squatting Kish with the mirror and has a big hit, then he passes it to Q. Meanwhile four American tourists (two middle-aged couples with binoculars) have poked their heads into the shed, wanting to buy coconuts. While Errol smoothly changes gears, addresses himself to the Americans, Q waves to him, slips away.

DAILY THRESHER

The Jah newspaper of highest repute is the Daily Thresher. Its politics evidently mimic those currently at the helm, which today is "conservative," after the distinguished twin models in the U.S. and the U.K.

Though the paper, editorially, is genteelly nationalistic, the prose is anglophile, with Latinate phrasings and unsupported references to "old boys," knighted civil servants, sporting Christianity.

The evidence shows, incidentally, that the British were less than sporting re their own brand of Christianity; the chattel Negroes were systematically discouraged from converting to High-Church Anglicanism. In this respect at least the British were notably unlike the proselytizing Spaniards.

From the Daily Thresher, a fragment of valedictory from "the number one" at Disraeli College:

> Fellow leavers: Disraeli has taught us many things, perhaps foremost of which is, as the American poet Hazlitt put it: "The awareness that the art of life is to know how to enjoy little and endure much."

AUTHOR

When Q looks in on Errol the next day at the same time, only the other Kish who was appraising his face in the hand-mirror is there. Yesterday he absolutely ignored Q; today he is effusive. He introduces himself as Dr. Feelgood and passes Q a spliff. Then he motions Q to squat with him on the grassy floor.

"Tell I what you wants, Johnny," he takes a big hit. "I gets it, no problem. My name is what I do, Dr. Feelgood. I wid de hunderworld. Mafia, politics, hit don't mean nothin, mon. Hit don't mean shit. Not fom de hinside."

Dr. Feelgood wears dark sunglasses with yellow frames. His hair is matted and piled high on his head. He is barechested, muscular with a small waist.

94

Q: "Maybe Errol told you. I'm here to meet Cudjoe."

F: "John Crow?"

Q: "Right. He's the Information Minister."

F: "Yah mon. I knows. I knows hall about de John Crow. You wants to meet wid he?"

Q: "Yes."

F: "You talkin bout de big money, Johnny."

Q: "What do you mean?"

F: "I means hit gone cos you meet wid im John Crow. . ."

The meeting is arranged for the following day, chez Errol. Meanwhile the power has gone off in Q's motel. Q, middle-aged, with a nagging pain in his lumbar, lies on his cot in coastal Jah. No water, no light.

ETHIOPIA

Sentient man appeared first in Ethiopia. Ritual celebrations honoring Deity, including prayer, animal sacrifice, testimonial music—occurred first in Ethiopia. So the Jah Kish maintain. The Kish even possess a "very early replica" of a long black reed nose-flute, which presumably produced the ritual music.

The scriptures are cited, Psalms 68:4, "Sing unto God, sing praises to his name: extol him that rideth upon the heavens by his name JAH, and rejoice before him."

And especially Psalms 68:31: "Princes shall come out of Egypt; Ethiopia shall soon stretch out her hands unto God."

Daniel 7:9 is cited: "The Ancient of Days did sit, whose garment was white as snow, and the hair of his head like the pure wool: his throne was like the fiery flame, and his wheels as burning fire."

"Pure wool" is, to the Kish, indisputable evidence that the Ancient of Days was Black, and Black was then synonymous with Ethiopian.

Sheba was of course Black, and it was through Solomon that the Scriptures first acknowledged Ethiopia; though, as indicated, Ethiopia's lineage is ancient as Adam.

More: Holy cannabis is praised in the Scriptures, according to the Jah Kish. Note Genesis 3:18; Exodus 10:12; Psalms 104:14; Proverbs 15:17.**

FAUNA

An alluring saurian: the five-to-seven-inch anole lizard, seen on verandas, fences, tree-trunks. Changes hue rapidly from green to brown to translucent ochre. Male tempts much smaller female by inflating its throat glands as much as three inches. Inflates, deflates, inflates . . . eight or ten times successively. Throat glands are of a different hue than the rest of him, alternating from yellow to orange to mahogany.

Goats graze everywhere, handsome piebalds with their doleful child-pitched "wah, waah." Will be slaughtered and made into curried goat for the rich. Neither goat's milk nor cheese eaten in Jah.

Hummingbirds: called "doctorbirds" because of their lancet-like beaks. The aggressive loggerhead kingbird: called "pechary" after its high-strung call. Patoo, also imitative, the commonest indigenous owl.

The ten-inch-in-diameter land crab of Dasheen emerges only at night from its woodland covert just east of the sea, scuttling across the ill-lit road to feed on tourists' garbage. They are run over by the speeding cars, then in the dawn fed upon by the turkey vultures.

The naked headed brown-black turkey vulture (*Cathartes aura*): known also as John Crow.

AUTHOR

Q is on time but Errol's shed is empty. A very old woman wants to know what Q is doing by "Errol premises."

"I have an appointment with Errol."

"Errol im haben is bart," she says. "Soon cum."

Fifty minutes later, Errol, fresh from the sea, sidles up to the shed, a large towel wrapped loosely about his dreads.

"The meeting?" Q wonders.

"Yah mon."

Errol squats on the floor, lights a spliff. Q also squats on the floor.

"Dr. Feelgood said—"

"Dr. Feelgood im no cum. Im associate cum."

"Cudjoe?"

Errol laughs. "Ow much you pay im Dr. Feelgood?" Q tells him.

"Dat too much, you know, bredda. Dr. Feelgood im use is brain on you. Ah, here Mr. Bone."

A large thick-legged man has lowered his head and enters the shed.

"I am," he says, "Mr. Bone," extending a massive thumbless hand.

Q shakes his hand. Errol passes him a spliff. Mr. Bone takes a sucky hit while with his other hand producing from somewhere a straight-backed chair: sits. He wears what looks like a sharkskin suit, navy blue, double-breasted, shiny from use, his fat thighs straining the seams. He is the first fat black man Q has seen in Jah.

Beneath his jacket Mr. Bone wears a white-on-white shirt, buttoned at the neck, but without a necktie. His large gold-plated cufflinks are Jah Kish in theme: a spherical ackee (Jah's national fruit) within an outline-map of Ethiopia.

Feeling disadvantaged at Mr. Bones's feet (Bone wears new-looking, high-top, black and white sneakers), Q stands. Mr. Bone has another hit.

Errol, his eyes lidded, the towel still about his head, squats on the grassy floor.

Above Mr. Bone, Q sees that he has conked or marcelled his hair.

B: "Dr. Feelgood send me."

Q: "What about Cudjoe?"

B: "Bone. My name is Mr. Bone."

Q glances at Errol who has re-entered his reverie.

Q: "Dr. Feelgood said he would put me in touch with

Cudjoe, Informa—"

Mr. Bone is holding up his thumbless hand. Q can see the thick seam where the primitive sutures were applied.

B: "You are from States?"

Q: "Yes."

B: "Philadelphia?"

Q: "California."

"Ah." Mr. Bone's deep voice turns sonorous. "The great San Francisco Earthquake. Nineteen ought six, was it not?"

"I suppose so. I couldn't say."

Errol has slipped through the burlap curtains into the small inner chamber. Q is standing above and to one side of Mr. Bone in the dim low-ceilinged room.

"I'm looking for Cudjoe, Information Minister of the John Crows," Q gets it out quickly.

Pause.

Mr. Bone is slowly swivelling his massive head, releasing a sweet strong smell of hair dressing. Gazing balefully up at Q through one red-rimmed, heavy-lidded eye:

"What white mon look fuh mean im nutin to John Crow."

SUB-TEXT (1)

—Did Q experience desire in Jah?

—Well, yes.

—Did Q consummate his desire?

—Do you recall Mavis, referred to earlier? The youthful higgler? Mavis sold Q a bottle of high-proof Jah rum for thirty-five pounds, a considerably higher than standard price, Q learned. Especially since the rum had been diluted with water. It was Mavis, then, who visited Q in his motel room on two consecutive rainy Dasheen late afternoons . . .

PATOIS

The cockney "h" that the Jah folk employ, inserting it before initial vowels, omitting it where it belongs, is actually based on West African models. It is variable: sometimes employed, other times not, even within the same sentence.

So too are the stunning eccentricities of usage, syntax and pitch based on West African models, which the Jahian clings to even as he reluctantly makes do with the colonial lingua franca.

THE DAILY THRESHER

From the letters:

> Sir:—An item appeared in your Sunday Thresher Magazine of 18 June 1984, under the heading "Signs, Symptoms of Scabies and Crabs," which described the Crab Lice as *Pediculosis Pubis.*
>
> My good and highly qualified friend, Mr. Nigel Dalloway, who for numerous years had great pleasure in calling me and all his other good chums a *Phthirus Pubis,* would be vexed if one of us did not step forward to correct the error.
>
> My information (Encyclopaedia Britannica, fourteenth ed.) is that *Pediculus Humanus* is the body lice, *Capitus Humanus,* the head lice, and *Phthirus Pubis* is the crab-like little fellow vigorously patrolling the groin (pubic) area.
>
> I am, etc.
>
> > Godfrey D. F. Parchment
> > Watchwell P.A.
> > St. Elizabeth
> > 12 July 1984

AUTHOR

Lights back on, but still no water in Q's motel. He bathes in the sea and uses the toilet in a nearby motel, or when that's not possible squats in the bush. No scarcity of bush, yet recently, squatting there just after dawn, he was stumbled upon by Quaco: the beginning of an acquaintanceship.

Quaco, handyman-cum-gardener at Q's blighted motel, actually caught Q's attention several days earlier when Q thought he heard him articulate the phrase "Creole Marxism" while talking with a Kish. Q made a mental note.

Quaco is, he says, thirty, short, with a long muscular torso and a nasty sutured-up slash that nearly spans his neck. He is bearded but with cropped hair—though sympathetic to the Kish he is not one. Q wonders whether he is a John Crow.

Once, after a typically fierce, but short-lived, late afternoon rain, Q and Quaco walk to the beach. Quaco lights a spliff, passes it to Q.

"You hear im de gunshots last night, bredda?"

"No."

They have turned east onto the sand. Crystalline sea, genial sun.

"De cops," Quaco says. "Dem shot dem an de beat dem. Yah bredda."

"Where?"

"Ere, bredda. Ere we be walkin. De cops dem kill de breddas."

"Why?"

"Sensi ganja. De cops dem say breddas dem grow de ganja. Hit's a lie, my bredda."

Q wants to be clear. "They beat them or they killed them?"

"Kill dem, bredda. De cops dem kill dem dead."

Quaco has another pull on his spliff, they walk in silence.

"You go to de reef, bredda?"

"What? No, I haven't been. It's pretty, I understand."

Quaco laughs. "Hit's bery pretty, you know, bredda. Jah

is bery pretty."
Q nods.
"You wants I take you in boat to de reef, bredda?"
"You have a boat?"
"Yah mon. A bredda im ave boat, you know. Cost you twenty pounds Jah, bery bery cheap."
Q grins.
"Same bredda im ave de best sensi ganja, mountain sensi. Im sells it to I, good price. You wants I sell it to you, my bredda? Bery good price."
Q laughs. Quaco laughs with him.
"You see ow de ocean look so pretty, bredda?"
Q nods.
"Wid dis sensi hit looks more pretty, you know. I sells it to you bery cheap because you my bredda."

GEOPOLITICAL
A large graffito on a wall in downtown Dasheen: SYRIAN, CHINEE OUT OF JAH!
Even in his brief time in Dasheen Q's seen the mercantile influence of these two groups. Between them they appear to own most of the large or middle-range stores, as well as the motels and villas. Q's own rundown motel is Chinese-owned.

PEOPLE, ETC.
Q has dinner at a small Kish outdoor restaurant. The Kish waiter emerges from the bush, approaching Q's table o-bliquely. And the waiter has stuffed only the foreparts of his bare feet into shoes, so that he shuffles comically as he walks. He is either hostile, neutral, or mildly friendly—Q can't tell which. He is humming (possibly satirically) what sounds like "Amazing Grace." And when he produces a rum bottle filled with water he says:
"Ere his your Kish Wine."
When the food finally comes it is saltless but peppery,

good: rice, beans, cassava bread, paw paw.

The Kish diet is regimented: roots, grain, legumes, mild fruit, but no meat and emphatically no pork. Of course the Kish are poor and when a Kish is very hungry and only the common inexpensive jerk-pork is available, he will call the pork "Arnold and then partake of it."**

SUB-TEXT (2)

The Kish outdoor restaurant is run by Molly, a slim blond Englishwoman in her early thirties. The ambiguous Kish waiter (note previous entry) is her husband and co-owner Cecil. They've been together nearly two years and have a child, Cufi. Cecil also has four other children by two previous wives, so a distraught Molly confides to Q.

Five days before, one day before Molly's thirty-fourth birthday, Cecil disappeared.

Q: "He took his motor scooter?"

M: "He must have. It's gone. Though I didn't hear it. We'd gone to bed, and when I awoke a few hours later to drink some water, he was gone."

Pause.

M: "It worries me because there are lots of people don't like Kish, you know."

Q: "This is the first time he's disappeared?"

M: "No, it's happened before. Though never for this long. And never before . . . my birthday. That sounds pouty, I know."

Q: "It doesn't."

M: "Yes, but we had been talking of doing something special for this birthday. Going—Cecil, Cufi, me—to Patu. I'm worried."

Q: "Of course."

M: "If this wasn't Dasheen I'd call the police, have them look for Cecil. Except they'd laugh at me."

Q: "Why?"

M: "Because I'm a pouty white female in Jah, and if I'm fool enough to marry a Kish then I must put up with his

102

foolishness. That's what they'd think while laughing at me."

Pause.

M: "There's something else, you know. I have no money to buy gas to cook on the stove. That's why the restaurant's been closed. Cecil loaned one of the brothers forty pounds and was supposed to get the money back a week ago."

Q: "He didn't get it back?"

M: "No. Not that I know of. If he's not back with some money by tomorrow, I won't be able to feed the child. That's what's really disturbing me. Because if I could, I'd leave tomorrow. Take Cufi and go. I can't handle this place anymore, I really can't. It's a paradise to look at, but underneath there's such a blackness . . . "

Q offers to lend Molly pounds. She says let's wait until tomorrow. Q drops in on her the next day, Cecil still has not come back, she still won't accept Q's money. Q comes by the following day; Cecil's come back, though he's not in at present.

Q: "What was it?"

Molly shrugs. "He was in Patu, doing Kish things with the brothers, he said."

Q: "The forty pounds?"

M: "Cecil brought back fifteen pounds. Just enough to light the stove and buy some things for tonight's dinner."

Q: "I'll be there."

M: "Good." A wan smile.

AUTHOR

Q anticipated miscues, even time-consuming and expensive ones. Dr. Feelgood was good theater but of no use. Ditto Mr. Bone. Q still has not given up on Errol, the name Q's contact expressly referred him to.

Q dropped by Errol's shed yesterday and waited there for about two hours without seeing him. Today, after his morning sea-bath, he tries again and Errol is in, squatting on the floor, sipping "roots" out of a fluted coca-cola glass.

Roots, a concept of broad application which includes at one extreme the Africanization of Jah, is also a potent non-alcoholic drink brewed from roots, tubers and other vegetable matter. It is iron red-brown in color.

"Ullo, my bredda."

"Hello, Errol."

"You hab find what you look?"

Q smiles. "No."

"I sorry fuh you, bredda. Mr. Bone im not elp?"

Errol is talking while sipping, not raising his head.

"Who is he, Errol? He didn't say a word about Cudjoe."

"Cudjoe? Oo you means?"

"I mean Mr. Bone."

"Ah, Bone, im Dr. Feelgood associate." Errol looks up from his drink. "Mr. Bone im Feelgood associate."

Q nods. "Well, Independence Day is Thursday, right?"

"Toorsday. Right you are, my bredda."

Errol sets his glass on the floor and lights up a spliff just a little smaller than an infant's arm. He passes it to Q.

"I told you it was important that I locate Cudjoe, didn't I, Errol?"

"Bery important, bredda. Dat what you say."

"But you can't lead me to him?"

"Ow much you pay im Dr. Feelgood?"

Errol asked him this the last time.

"Hundred-fifteen pounds Jah," Q says. "But I thought that was for a meeting with Cudjoe. All I got was Mr. Bone."

"Mr. Bone im bery smart man, you know, bredda."

DAILY THRESHER

With reference to the upcoming 20th anniversary of Independence, this veiled plea to the "First World" countries in the Thresher leader:

The rich man by all the standards of a civilized society was not a cruel man of violent passions. He was merely indifferent to the beggar's presence. This was his real sin, a serious failure to notice suffering in his human brother.

PEOPLE

On the beach a higgler, a ragged boy of about fourteen, stops in front of three nude American girls lying on their stomachs abreast, and tries to sell them a Norman Rockwell reproduction with the heading: DO UNTO OTHERS AS YOU WOULD HAVE THEM DO UNTO YOU: a disparate collection of folk at prayer: two black children, an East Indian-looking girl, a Chinese child carrying the Wheel of the Law, an ancient rabbinical Jew with his Torah, a kindly white-skinned nun with a swarthy infant in her arms . . .

The girls finally slip into their bikinis and leave the beach, persistent boy at their heels.

BELIEF

Even as the African-inspired Vodun, in Haiti, and Shango, in Trinidad, have modified the indigenous belief systems, helped produce an amalgam of Shamanism, Totemism and Christianity; so has Kumina (Ashanti) altered Kish, in Jah—perhaps beyond the ken of pink, tenacious, short-armed Q.

Re John Crow: Q's information was that the abiding conflict between secular- and theocratic-based insurrection recently shifted in the direction of the secular, among whom Cudjoe was a leading advocate.

QUACO

Q buys three fat spliffs from Quaco, and, for twenty pounds Jah, has Quaco row him out to the reef where they snorkel on the transparent blue-green still surface, peering down at the multiform chaos . . .

In the boat again Quaco lights a spliff and lies on his back across the stern.

"Quaco," Q says, "the other day I thought I heard you use the term 'Creole Marxism.' "

Quaco on his back gives a wide grin. "Yah mon. You like hit?"

"What does it mean?"

Quaco takes another hit and passes the spliff to Q. Then he sits up. "Hit means history." Suddenly he seems intensely serious. He pokes himself hard in the chest with two fingers. "Hit mean Jah history, what work fuh we."

"Does it have to do with John Crow?"

"Yah mon. John Crow im Jah. Hab tuh do wid all Jah."

"Does it have to do with white, rich, Syrian, Chinese?"

But Quaco has slipped overboard and underwater; Q feels him tug at the anchor which must not have settled securely. Quaco hoists himself back on board effortlessly and again lies across the stern. He motions Q to pass him the spliff.

On his back with his spiky beard jutting up, his eyes closed, Quaco resembles photos Q has seen of the martyred Patrice Lumumba.

Silence.

Quaco takes another hit with a lot of air; he says to Q:

"What you looks fuh, bredda? You don come a Dasheen fe de sun, fe de sensi."

Q is thinking how to respond to this, when Quaco says:

"Hi knows what you come to the country of Jah fuh, bredda. Hi knows it and Hi sings it fuh you, my bredda."

Humming, Quaco establishes a Puku beat, then, tapping his knee with two fingers:

> Poor, rich, black, white, Chinee,
> Us all in de soup to-ged-da.
> Black, white, rich, poor, Chinee,
> Us all in de same pocky soup.

FAUNA

The familiar symbiosis between kine and cattle egret (*Bubulus ibis*): white long-legged bird mounted on the grazing bull, dislodging lice and fleas, is more prevalent in Jah than anywhere Q's been.

It is an emblem.

Of what?

PEOPLE

Q, gazing at the sunset, was sitting on a rock in the vegetation bordering the sand, when two girls appeared, one carrying a naked infant, and began silently to finger the ground directly beneath him.

Q stood and moved back. Neither girl looked more than fourteen or fifteen. They bent pliantly, moving their fingers under and around the large rock where Q had been sitting.

"What is it?" Q articulated the words distinctly. "What are you looking for?"

At this the girl without the infant looked up and granted him a radiant though impersonal smile.

"Wild thyme," she said. "For de baby, im sick."

"Wild thyme?" Q said.

The girl was still smiling, shyly. "We makes a tea."

Just then the other girl, the mother, made a sound and began to pull at the grass. The first girl joined her. Deftly, rapidly, they gathered a small bunch of purple-tipped grass and were about to leave.

"Let me smell it," Q said.

The young mother held the wild thyme up to his nose.

"It not smells," she said.

It didn't.

INDEPENDENCE

The annual celebration in Jah west always takes place in the soccer stadium in Patu, where Q stopped briefly en route to Dasheen. Puku bands and fireworks and rum and ganja, and—Errol indicated in Q's most recent interview with him—Brother Cudjoe or another high-level John Crow to address the crowd.

Though there are a number of white tourists in Dasheen, Q is the only white on the bus to Patu, and once in Patu, fifty minutes away: not another caucasian in sight. Eight-twenty p.m., Patu brimming with celebrants, including a surprising number of Kish wearing their colors: red, black and green. Red for spilled innocent blood dating from the first colonial intrusion into Africa. Black for the predominant hue of the Jah citizenry. Green for both the magical Caribbean and dense vegetation.**

Q on the bus, observes this stunning like-mindedness: with competing music and much other noise from a hundred different sources, nearly everyone is dancing: in the streets, shops, outdoor market, *in their bus seats*: young, old, both sexes, Kish. Not literally dancing, but swaying their bodies in dance, doing whatever they're doing, while fluidly maintaining the rhythm—maintaining everywhere the same rhythm.

The Patu football stadium, named after one of the early black liberators, is large, badly run-down. Q estimates that at least two thousand people are standing on the turf facing the bandstand, listening to an elderly politician praise Jah. His peroration . . . his leavetaking . . . scattered applause, increasing as a Puku band with Kish dreadlocks capers onto the bandstand. Even as the snappy MC introduces them (they're called Jah-Free) they can scarcely be contained—and then they're doing it and everyone is really dancing.

Though Q has been in Jah for nearly three weeks, only now, watching the dancing Jahians on the broken turf on every side of him, does he see how *African* they are: their heads, their carriage, their distinctive suppleness. The insight stirs Q—further estranging him.

The stadium is filling rapidly; still Q does not spot a single other caucasian. The entertainment is either music or patriotic oratory. And so far no sign of John Crow (who, in the photos Q has seen, was always dressed in Castro-like fatigues).

Q has received numerous questioning looks, stares, glares, and a handful of smiles too; but now something odd is happening. Five rough-looking teenage boys standing a-breast have angled closer to where he is standing, close enough so that one of them is brushing Q's shoulder. Another Puku group is doing its thing onstage and the teenage boys are sort of swaying along with everyone else, only their faces are utterly expressionless, and now the one who was brushing Q is leaning on him.

Abruptly, Q moves back, then sidles closer to the bandstand. Meanwhile, a uniformed John Crow has taken his seat on the platform and is about to be introduced. Wrong; he is an officer in the Jah army and will obviously be delivering yet another patriotic address . . . Yes, he refers to the Prime Minister, then expresses his gratitude to "United States officials" for their "moral and material support as we prepare to move stalwartly into our third decade of independence . . . " Again the teenage boys have moved alongside Q, their bodies still pliantly swaying, their faces impassive as masks. Only this time they are standing on either side of Q, very close.

Again Q changes position, this time moving back, then farther back into the crowd. He is relieved that they do not follow him. He continues watching the bandstand while staying alert to the people around him. He notices some Jah-ians reading a notice on a wooden stake, then sees that it is a hand-printed program. In fact wooden stakes with programs are planted here and there throughout the stadium. Scanning one, Q sees that there is no mention of Cudjoe or any other John Crow.

Q remains for another fifteen or twenty minutes, then makes his way outside, where after some time he squeezes into a Dasheen-bound bus. When Q reaches into his pocket for the fare, his wallet is gone.

SUB-TEXT (3)

—Q concedes that he has come to Jah for "personal reasons." Amplify.

—It is not so much a concession as a statement of fact.

—And Q has experienced desire in Jah?

—Naturally.

—May we assume that this elusive Creole Marxism that middle-aged Q is stalking is a resolution of his thwarted desire?

—I don't know what "resolution" means in the sense you use it. If you mean compensation, the answer is no. No.

AUTHOR

Q's wallet was gone, but his passport and credit cards, as well as nearly 200 pounds Jah, were fortunately secreted in his suitcase.

Errol puts Q in contact with an older Kish called Das at the northern tip of Dasheen, who, after a shared spliff and 90 pounds Jah, informs Q that Cudjoe, the Information Minister of the John Crows, is in the port city of St. Ives on the opposite coast of the island.

Q: "Are you certain of this?"

Das: "Yah mon."

FROM THE DAILY THRESHER

Jah's Prime Minister, the Rt. Hon. Clifton Glossop, is to head a committee to redesign the traditional Jah Coat of Arms to (in the Prime Minister's words) "befit the aspirations of our people within the framework of our national heritage, especially during this landmark summer."

The traditional Coat of Arms, initially granted in 1661 under the Royal Warrant of Charles the Second, contains four pineapples, an idealized aboriginal, and a crocodile rampant against the Royal British Crown.

However, as Prime Minister Glossop aptly put it: "Our pineapple is a minor crop, the aboriginal is extinct, and the crocodile is scarcely dignified."

The Committee to Redesign the Jahian Coat of Arms (CRJCA) promises to present an alternative, "more dignified design," within the fortnight.

ENVOI
We are in the New Abyssinia National Bank. Observe Q, discouraged but undaunted, middle-aged, freckly with sun, stiff in the lumbar, drawing on his MasterCard for Jah pounds, so that he can bus to St. Ives on the East Coast of the island, in continued pursuit of Brother Cudjoe of the John Crows.

* Here and hereafter, the asterisk refers to Frederic C. Cassidy's invaluable *Jamaica Talk: Three Hundred Years of the English Language in Jamaica* (Macmillan Caribbean: London, 1971).

**Leonard Barrett, *The Rastafarians: Sounds of Cultural Dissonance* (Beacon Press: Boston, 1977). See also Barrett's *Soul-Force: African Heritage in Afro-American Religions* (New York, 1974).

THREE

MONKEY

"No fucking legs, man!"

Laura and Nigel and Gretchen stared at Henry across the round oak table. The sun was going down. Laura was pouring the wine.

"Again," Gretchen said.

Henry thrust out his arms in a furious gesture: "No fucking legs, man!"

Pause.

"Let me try," Laura said, setting down the bottle. "A legless Vietnam vet responding to a question at one of those Agent Orange protest camps in California."

Laura was married to Henry, Nigel to Gretchen. It was the fifth time the couples had met socially.

Nigel: "What was the question and who asked it?"

"A local reporter asked the question," Laura said. "It was: 'From this point in time, what does the Vietnam War mean to you, and how has it changed your lifestyle?' "

Gretchen and Nigel looked at Henry.

"That's about right," Henry said.

"The 'how has it changed your lifestyle' is good," Gretchen said.

"She's very shrewd," Nigel said.

"I know my husband," Laura said. She picked up the bottle and poured the rest of the wine into Gretchen's glass. (Laura: thirty-four, slender, high-strung, with a mane of black hair, shining green eyes, a wide plastic mouth.)

"Do you?" Nigel said.

"What?"

"Know your husband?"

Laura looked across at Henry who kept a straight face. "Not like the palm of my hand," she said. "I know what's eating him, though. It's what's eating me."

"Hmm," from Nigel.

"You're Monkey, Gretchen," Laura said.

"I am?"

"Yes, we're moving counter-clockwise around the table."

They were sitting in the kitchen, a wide old room with cedar wainscoting and a wood stove in the corner. A fluted ceramic vase of white lilacs stood on the stove.

Gretchen (with a slim forefinger on the top of her nose): "Let me think. All right: Qua! Qua! Qua! Quaah!"

"I know," Nigel said. "A middle-aged matron at a neighborhood Chinese restaurant. She's just choked to death on a bit of barbecued spare rib."

Chuckles.

"Not even close," Gretchen said.

Pause.

"Do it again, Gretchen," Laura said.

Gretchen had a sip of wine, then, widening her mouth: "Aii! Aii! Aii! Aii! Aii-oww!"

"That isn't what you said before," Nigel said. "Before it was 'qua,' now it's 'ai.' "

Gretchen shrugged. Early forties, with a strong high-boned face and thick brown hair flecked with gray, tied in a pony tail.

"An animal," Laura said. "A harp seal pup about to be clubbed to death by a Canadian fur murderer."

Gretchen looked at Laura admiringly. "You're really tuned in, Laura."

"Laura is our connoisseur of chaos," Nigel said. "Shall I fetch more wine?"

"Do," Henry said. "In the pantry."

"That was very close to what I meant, Laura."

"What did you mean?"

"Dolphins, netted then piked to death on a beach by Japanese fishermen."

Nigel, standing, with a fresh bottle of California Cabernet in one hand and the corkscrew in the other: "I wasn't really that far off, was I? Chinese restaurant, Japanese fishermen." Thickset, with bushy salt-and-pepper beard and cool brown eyes behind bifocals, Nigel had been a solicitor in the U.K. and was now a lit. prof. in the U.S. Working the corkscrew into the Cabernet.

The night before a battalion of American marines landed in Honduras near the Nicaraguan border, and on that same night the Iranians scored a direct hit with their Israeli-made missile on a Kuwaiti tanker carrying American oil; the Persian Gulf near Kharg Island was on fire. This morning (in an "unrelated development") the Secretary of Defense confirmed that the new U.S. "posture" would no longer exclude a first nuclear strike and re-emphasized that a "limited nuclear war" was indeed "winnable."

Nigel sniffed the cork then sat down. "Why don't we let it breathe for a bit."

Henry nodded.

"I'm not sure I like this game," Nigel said. "It's called Monkey, is it?"

Laura nodded. "Henry got it from Simone Weil."

Nigel: "The French-Jewish fanatic?"

Laura: "One must strive to limit those evils that are not inseparable from the human condition."

Nigel: "Who said that?"

Laura: "Simone Weil."

Nigel: "Not surprised. Very high-toned. What does it have to do with Monkey?"

Henry: "An inmate in Treblinka, a woman subsequently executed there, had kept a diary which was smuggled out and Simone Weil had a look at it. Monkey was evidently something the inmates did when they had a free minute. Possibly it established a small distance—or at least irony— between the inmates and their fate there."

Henry was Laura's age, slight of build, with a full red beard and expressive features. Friends said he resembled D. H. Lawrence. Henry's field, like his wife's, was Theater-Arts.

Nigel raised the open bottle to the light and shook his head slowly. "During the Blitz we read, you see. I read all of Smollett. I was only nine or ten, mind you. It was the most vivid reading I've ever done."

Laura: "Are you saying the Treblinka inmates might have spent their final hours more fruitfully by reading Smollett?"

"Smollett is a gas," Nigel, wryly.

"Have some more wine, love." Gretchen picked up the bottle.

Nigel held up his hand. "Not yet. Best let it breathe for a while longer. My turn?"

Henry nodded.

Nigel pointed to the east window. "Lovely. Full moon. Even whilst the sun is fading. Is that a hickory tree just outside?"

"Pignut hickory," Henry said.

"Lovely," Nigel said.

"Tonight we will hear the mockingbird," Gretchen said.

"Will the mockingbird sing tonight in Nicaragua?" Laura said.

"Isn't there a story by Malamud called 'Jewbird'?" Nigel said.

"I think there is," Henry said.

Nigel: "That might have been a better name for this game than Monkey. Since it came out of Treblinka, you know."

Gretchen: "Bad taste, pet. Very Goon-Show."

"How solemn we all are," Nigel said. "All right, my turn." In a southern drawl:

Yawl contend that Bubba dint do wrong.
The State contend that Bubba guilty as the day is long,
That if Bubba dint go there with no evil on his mind,
How come the boy done left his smokin .357 Magnum behind?

The State make its case both loud and clear:
The boy Claudell was shot dead behind his left ear
with a single round from a .357 Magnum,
Which just happens to be the defendant Bubba's gun;

And futha-more, for some time Claudell had been makin
Fast and loose with Bubba's mistress,
Which give us the motive and this we stress:
Bubba done murdered Claudell, shot him behind the left ear,

And the State be askin for death, or at the very least,
Two hundred and ninety-nine year.

Henry laughed.

"You've outdone yourself," Gretchen said.

"Yes, but will it scan?"   '

"It won't scan, Nigel," Laura said.

"Sounds like a state prosecutor," Henry said. "Mississippi?"

"Very good, Henry. North Carolina, actually. I saw it in the *Times* a month or so back. An old bloke from somewhere in Carolina. He routinely summarizes the state's case in this sort of doggerel."

"Bubba and Claudell," Gretchen said. "That's very good."

"Bubba was real," Nigel said. "Claudell was my invention."

"Hurrah for your invention," Laura said. She picked up the bottle, poured wine all around.

"You're altogether too somber, Laura."

119

"You make it sound like an indisposition after a British lawn party," Laura said. "I'm pissed. I'm among the millions in this country who are pissed."

"Pity," Nigel said.

"Nigel lived through the Blitz," Gretchen said. "Nothing since has measured up."

Nigel: "What's a military invasion of Nicaragua, or even some radioactive dispersion, that a grand sunset in May can't dispel?"

"Now that scans," Laura said. "It would sound even 'grander' if you were wearing your public school tie."

"What else do you find grand besides sunsets, Nigel?" Henry asked.

"Love is grand," Nigel said. "Drink is grand."

"Nigel is very good at drink," Gretchen said.

Smiles from Henry, Laura.

"You're so much more appealing when you smile," Nigel said to Laura. "But don't listen to me. I'm a bit tipsy. I think I've drunk more than the rest of you. Yes, I like my grog, and I like a bit of fucking now and again. Of course I'm British and doubtless a bit opaque, but what does this game mean? This Jewbird, or Monkey, as you call it?"

Just then Garbo, Laura and Henry's large Manx leaped onto the table and began to whine. Henry picked her up and put her outside. While Henry was standing Laura shifted from her chair to his. Nigel wondered why.

"It's begun to rain," Henry said.

"Too bad," Gretchen said.

"How about some music?" Nigel said.

"What's your pleasure?" Henry said.

"Something bonny."

"We have no Elgar. Delius?"

"Wasn't he a syphilitic?" Nigel said.

"Boccherini then? We have some very nice Boccherini."

"By the way, Laura, these Windsor chairs are handsome. Late 18th century, no?"

Laura nodded.

"Just a bit rugged on the arse. If you don't mind my saying so."

"Nigel has a bony coccyx," Gretchen said.

Nigel: "Vestigial tail, I suppose it is."

"Henry," Laura called. "Bring in a cushion for Nigel's vestigial tail."

"Back to the game," Nigel said. "Whose turn?"

"Laura's," Gretchen said.

Henry came back into the kitchen, handed Nigel an embroidered green cushion and sat down in the chair Laura had vacated.

Laura, explosively: "Get your damn hands off of me! And leave my father alone, damn you! I told you before my name is Karen Smith and not Chesimard!"

Pause.

Nigel: "That's very nice Boccherini. Sounds to me as if some Mafiosi got their hands on the wrong people."

"Not Mafiosi," Gretchen said. "Police. This was in the papers just a while ago. The police got a tip that Joanne Chesimard, who's a fugitive and black, was seen on some expressway in New York. So they arrested this woman Karen Smith *and* her father. Karen Smith is a dozen years younger than Chesimard and they look nothing alike."

Nigel: "What was the charge?"

"Resisting arrest," Gretchen said. "I think she's still in prison."

"Out on bail," Laura said.

Nigel: "The police have ascertained that she isn't in fact the fugitive?"

"Right," Laura said. "The charge—resisting arrest—still stands."

"I see," Nigel said. "Your blacks are up against it, aren't they? I'm rather hungry. What if I went out for some crisps or something?"

Henry stood. "How about some dried fruit and nuts?"

"Eh? Dried fruit? I was thinking about something a bit more piquant."

121

"We'll be eating in about an hour," Gretchen said.

Henry, opening the refrigerator: "We've gone one round. Now the game becomes collaborative."

Nigel: "Collaborative? We're all to collaborate with each other? Sort of randomly?"

"Nigel is polysexual," Gretchen said.

"You mean polymorphous, dear."

"Those British public schools!" Henry shook his head. He set a wooden bowl of nuts and fruit on the table, stroked his wife's hair, sat down.

Laura, through pursed lips, with appropriate Tory cadence: "The supple rod in thin long hands applied to pale trembling loins."

Smiles.

"Best not to mock what you've never tried," from Nigel.

"Caning is uplifting," Gretchen said.

"Now don't let's give away too much, dear. Tell us about the collaboration, Henry."

"It's a version of that surrealist game called 'Exquisite Corpse.' Man Ray, Breton, Duchamp, Claudel, that crowd, did collaborative drawings and verse and one of the phrases they came up with was 'The exquisite corpse drinks the young wine.' In our instance we can call the game Exquisite Monkey."

"How does it go then?"

"One of us begins," Henry said. "The rest of us in turn continue the narrative by supplying a sentence or two or some brief dialogue."

Nigel: "The theme, I take it, remains War and Destitution?"

Laura: "The theme is How It Seems to You."

Nigel: "And is that all there is to it?"

Henry: "What more would you like?"

Nigel: "Don't know. Something for the victor, maybe. I should think a bit of exquisite nooky would—"

Laura: "No winners in this game."

"There is of course," Henry pointed out, "a kind of vying

122

from within. From within the narrative."

"Sounds very bonny," Nigel said. "Who's to begin?"

"Why don't you," Gretchen said.

"All right. Four middle-aged, middle-class, middling successful university types are sitting on antique Windsor chairs about an oak table in an artsy kitchen sipping middling California red out of Art Deco wine goblets."

Laura: "At least one of them is thinking about the bag-lady who has recently taken to living—sprawled behind her bags and boxes—on the university grounds."

Gretchen: "Someone gave her a coin and asked her name. She just shook her head."

Henry: "Eventually she will make her way to our country's capitol where she will join tens of thousands of other homeless people in Lafayette Park, across from the White House."

Nigel: "They will drink beer and play skittles and bitch when they're drunk and moan when they lose."

Laura: "A: 'How come there's so many goddamn beggars in the park?' B: 'Why, they're setting up a tent city. They call it Reaganville.' "

Gretchen: "The scrawl on the toilet-paper dispenser in an outhouse in Tent City: 'REAGANOMICS AT WORK!' "

Henry: "Park Cop: 'What they trying to prove?'

Local: 'They want a fair shake, is all.'

Cop: 'Where they think they at? Oz? Ain't but one shake. And it ain't fair. It ain't nothin.' "

Nigel got up, went into the living room, turned over the Boccherini, then came back into the kitchen.

"Boccherini reminds me of victuals. Some northern Italian would do very nicely."

"Laura's already made reservations, pet. For seven-thirty."

"At Trattoria Luigi?"

"At Gloria's," Gretchen said.

"Not health food!"

"Healthful food, love. Vegetarian and fish. I told you we

123

were eating at Gloria's. You forgot."

"Doesn't go with Boccherini. You should have played us an Indian raga, Henry. Or something jingly from Vietnam."

"Jingly is Indonesia," Laura said. "Not Vietnam."

"It's not too late," Henry said. "Shall I play an evening raga?"

"Let's stay with the Boccherini." Nigel checked his watch. "Another round?" Laura said.

"Now I know how you keep imperially slim, Laura. You feed on your own gall."

"Now Nigel," Gretchen said.

"Name a country," Laura said, "that has proceeded from barbarism to decadence without the intervening stage of civilization."

"The U.S. of A.," Gretchen said.

Smiles.

"I see a difference between playing at commitment and being committed," Nigel said.

"As I see it," Henry said, "Monkey is an exhibition of feeling. Feeling is preliminary to acting."

"It's raining harder," Gretchen said. "Can you hear it?"

"What sort of acting are we talking about, Henry?"

"Well, there's a wide gamut, isn't there? From leafletting, to fasting, to marching, to resisting with force."

"Probably we should leave earlier," Gretchen said. "For Gloria's."

Laura went to the door and let in the cat, wet and whining. She opened the refrigerator and took out a plastic container of cat food. While she was standing Henry slipped from his chair into hers.

"Wouldn't you agree," Nigel said, "that virtually none of the bourgeois intellectuals who exhibit their feelings in their bourgeois fastnesses will do anything beyond exhibiting their feelings?"

"Under ordinary circumstances, I agree," Henry said. "But when people understand, as I think they've come to understand, that their lives and especially their children's

124

lives are endangered by the crass and willful ignorance of those in charge—then the circumstances are no longer ordinary."

"Rather obscene, isn't it?" Nigel went on. "This playing at commitment. An insult to those in the front lines, I should say."

"In Vietnam, most of those in the front lines were poor or colored and would rather not have been there," Henry said. "Would you expect it to be any different in Central America?"

"The obscenity," Laura, sitting down in Henry's vacated seat, said, "is in the pretense that nothing has really changed. That the world is as it's been, with its unequal portions of misery and cruelty. And that since the world has, after its fashion, survived, it will continue to survive."

Nigel filled up his glass with wine and drank half of it in one swallow. "I should call this faith rather than obscenity."

Gretchen got up and went into the bathroom. It was raining harder. Branches of the hickory tree lashed the window. The rain pelting the house made an odd metallic sound like the beating on a snare drum.

"Are you secure in your faith that the U.S. will not initiate a nuclear first-strike?" Henry said. "Or that the U.S. will not provoke the faithless Soviet Union to initiate such a strike? Or that one of a dozen 'third world' countries won't blow off their new bomb at some provocation or other?"

The bathroom was off the kitchen. They could hear Gretchen peeing. Garbo, the Manx, hopped onto Gretchen's chair and, purring hoarsely, proceeded to groom herself.

"I'm secure in my faith that North Americans are possessed of a millenarian neurosis which has continued to one degree or another since your Roundheads wrested the country from the Indians—and then fell to the ground and prayed for deliverance."

Gretchen returned to the table and, standing over her chair, stroked the cat.

Laura: "I had no idea you were so mulish, Nigel. You

ought to run for Congress. I know you're not an American citizen, but once the Republican party chieftains hear you out they would probably waive that requirement."

"Touché, Laura." Nigel gave a wide smile which uncovered an uneven row of pebbly teeth. "I'm mulish, as you say, but I'm not necessarily wrong. And I'm lovable."

Gretchen: "I think he means that he is not necessarily lovable and he is wrong."

"I should like to convince you otherwise, Laura," Nigel said.

Laura made a sound from deep in her throat. Henry stood. He went to the door.

"It's going to rain this way for a while," he said. "Why don't we get going?"

Laura stood and went to Henry. She put a slender long arm about his waist.

"I'll get our jackets," Gretchen said.

"Turn off the record player, Gretchen," Henry said.

Now Laura had one arm around her husband's neck and the other on his hip. Her front was pressed against his back. She was a bit taller than he, but they were built along the same lines and seemed almost like sister and brother.

Henry turned suddenly and kissed his wife on the mouth.

Laughing softly, Laura tossed her head.

Now both their backs were turned toward Nigel, who, still seated, continued to drink his wine, looking at them.

SIDEWINDER

"Neither shalt thou stand against the blood
of thy neighbor."

Leviticus 19:16

They were massed at the volleyball net. G supposed they
were Palestinians.

Ich hab ein glühend Messer / I have a glowing knife

They could have been Jordanians, Syrians, Iraquis—or any
combination of these. Except that a certain scruffy, keen-
eyed homogeneity spelled Palestinian. Young men in their
twenties, most of them short, with tightly curled hair, black
shiny eyes, quick, clever jerky movements: they laughed
and shouted in Arabic and smacked the white rubber ball.

Ich hab
ein glühend
Messer

G was jogging. The volleyball net—with its two dozen capering Palestinians—was set on the grass approximately in
the center of the quarter-mile track. G had jogged before Israel decided to bomb Beirut (with the declared intention of
smoking out every last Palestinian guerrilla). He jogged

127

while Israel was bombing. And he jogged when Israel at last ceased to bomb: thousands

killed, many thousands wounded, the once-graceful city in rubble. Only a very small number of those killed and maimed

glühend Messer
glühend Messer

could have been Palestinian guerrillas. The casualties were mostly Lebanese, old and young. Of course much of the country had been in rubble before the bombing. Nor had the fratricidal war (Muslim against Falangist Christian) ever ceased. So cited the apologists, themselves Jewish, since few non-Jews ever truly empathized with Jew-as-Victim, and virtually none would identify with Jew-as-Agressor. Is this true? Does it matter here in the twisted bowel of

Messer Messer Messer Messer

holocaust? Flatfooted, thin-haired, middle-aged G jogging around the university track, the uneven quarter-mile dirt circle reserved for amateurs. Another synthetic-surfaced, meter-lined track just above him to the north was reserved for the supple-limbed, quasi-moronic jocks. Correction: they are not quasi-moronic. They are

Ich hab
Ich hab
Ich hab

Southern Californians, female and male. Slender, pliant, blond. G knew beauty but did not possess it. He lectured on Art History to these same non-moronic blonds, tanned and languid and filling the classroom like a mild odorless wind. G's windowless classrooms never smelled of body. In the

fourteen years G had lectured on Art he did not recall smell-
ing a single wayward fart or menses. Nor were the breaths
of these youths ever stale and many

very many believed powerfully in Jesus. Until the last two or
three years there had been *no* Palestinians. There was of
course the perennial phalanx of high-caste un-white: from
India, Pakistan, Saudi Arabia, from pre-Khomeini Iran, a
handful with their tribal scars from Nigeria. This small
quantity among a student body of thirty-five thousand
made no impact on G. But Jews were kindly then. No, that's
not it. Hear me: Jew will not equal

Ich   hab ein glühend Messer

Israel. Besides, Israel killed back differently then. Killed
then stopped. Stopped after killing. Stopped.

Did not supply advanced weaponry to South Africa, to
Argentina, to fascist Guatemala with its born-again
Generalisimo. G was jogging (flatfooted, slightly stooped,
balding), his mind working. Twenty-five or thirty Palestinians capering in the grassy center. Ten past five on a Saturday. G and a thirtyish woman the only joggers. But then
two Palestinians separated from the others, commenced to
jog. They ran past G with their untamed hair and odd awk-
ward gaits, chatting loundly in Arabic, one wearing a too-
strong cologne. One and a half circuits around the track and
they faded back into the mass at the net. And now the
woman jogger was done. She was mounting the stone
steps. (This field—both track and grassy playing area—was
recessed like an amphitheatre.) G, into his third plodding
mile, watched them grab at each other in play, leap for the
ball, even hit it with their heads, shout in Arabic, the guttural syllables like salvos of gunfire in the fragrant air. G
jogged around their perimeter, they

didn't seem to notice him. G had argued with his wife. Otherwise "liberal," she would not own up to Israel's bombs. When G handed her a newspaper piece detailing another lethal sortie into Lebanon, she would read it without reading it. On one of the few times when G persisted beyond reason she exploded: "Israel is not

alone! Moreover they're up against it. So they bomb. But then they all bomb." When the bombing began G was lecturing on Goya. Three or four of his keener students saw in the physical attitude of the executioners in Goya's "The Third of May" (projected onto the darkened wall) draftsmanship, composition, application of paint. Ethics (unalloyed with

Messer	*Messer*
Messer	*Messer*
Messer	*Messer*

applied Christianity) made them skittish, these languid, pliant blonds. G was huffing around the track, the Palestinians capering at the net. The bombing had paused for three days when a chief Rabbi of someplace (not in Israel) threatened to "excommunicate" any Jew who dared criticize the Blitz. G for

Goldstein, of course. His side ached, his mind worked. The Palestinians came only on Saturdays, between five and six o'clock. While the American students were showering in their fraternity houses, pointing to dinner and sex and driving fast and beer and bong and sex, twenty-five or thirty curly-haired Palestinians in shorts or sweatsuits began almost imperceptibly to congregate. As soon as half a dozen are at the net the game gets under way: smacking the ball, using their heads, laughing, heckling each other . . . As their number swells the game continues. It seems to G that the two sides never actually compete, just random joyous smacking. G did something

Ich hab ein glühend   Messer

uncharacteristic after the bombing picked up, the casualties mounted. He met a Chicana who recognized (somehow) his need, who for a price manacled him and while the bombing

crossed behind his back, G had met her where one meets such: she saw she accommodated him, it was the first time anything like this (remotely like this), G felt no guilt, felt cleansed

almost, twice now on the three previous Saturdays G was the sole jogger while the Palestinians capered at the net, sun low in the sky, waxing scimitar moon, pungent eucalyptus, killdeers shrieking. G's colleagues were formalists, endorsing more or less the prevailing academic dogma that *to create*

Ich hab ein Ich hab ein Ich hab ein Ich

"is an intransitive verb," that heart is outmoded utterly, that energy is indeed matter, that what matters above all is the language or paint in the artist's skull, that the most impressive craniums belong not to artists but to commentators on art. G was alone on the track

and off. Blond sun fading. She phoned him the following week at his office, said: "Eet eez your commander speaking." She had wit, G shouldn't have given her his number, one lunatic parenthesis was enough, still he was tempted a second time, he didn't do it, he was

MesserMesserMesserMesser

Goldstein. The ball got loose. G stopped jogging to retrieve it, tossed it back, one of the Palestinians nodded his head, two or three others glanced at him as if seeing him for the first time. The fact is that last night Israel resumed its annihilation of Beirut after nearly a week's pause. Gray shining moon-blade in the east, distinctly cooler. G's wife would blame it on History. Ingenuity,

she'd say sadly, was one of the few trump cards that Devil History dealt the Jews. Thus Israel's lethal technology. It was cold and G sweated. He did not wish to trivialize his wife's position. She did feel something for the dark-skinned victims, though *in vacuo*, unattached to the specific oppression. She in turn insisted that G was inclined to wink at non-Israeli oppressions, especially when they came from the non-white Left. G would wink at these, yet agonize and beat his breast over Israel. Was this true? In fact Israel's oppressions did evoke in G a particular shame. Was this unreasonable? Was his wife's hair-splitting reasonable in the stench of fratricide? These semitic Muslims are our blood. These frail children and pregnant mothers and mute elderly are our

Ich hab ein (glühend) Messer

blood.

Pine and eucalyptus and palm. 110-foot-high blue gum eucalyptus all about the track's perimeter. Sharply pungent. How is the sparse root-water pumped to the tips of the uppermost branches? G knows. Co-

hesion, the "intermolecular attraction that makes water particles stick to one another." Keen-edged moon now etched in the sky. Eucalyptus leaves on the dirt track. G has already jogged farther than usual, though at his usual lumbering pace. The woman jogger left twenty minutes ago, climbed the steep stone steps leading onto the campus proper. G was counting the Palestinians . . . Twenty-six at the net, with their intense jerky movements, their voices carrying in the cool early evening, the guttural Arabic words pitched high into the too-pungent air. With the sun over the horizon, the breeze (out of the east) picks up, wafting the stiff elongated eucalyptus leaves to the ground like knives, like (in a Neruda poem) "dead knives." Like

> *ein glühend*   *Ich*
> *hab*
> *ein glühend*

the dry stiff bodies of old Lebanese women. He was counting the Palestinians; their jerky uncalculated movements in and out of the mass, along with their (to G) virtual indistinguishability, made counting them difficult. Between twenty-two and twenty-eight young Palestinian men at the net. She

had the "equipment" herself, in her scuzzy room above the laundromat, crossed behind his back, trussed-up on the floor at her boots, she praised him afterwards, said he was good a

good boy. But what about the rest of the time, now, when I'm *man*, witness? G is counting the Palestinians when the ball rolls loose onto the track where he retrieves it. Except instead of tossing it back he resumes his slow flatfooted jog holding the ball. After an astonished pause,

> *MesserMesserMesser*   *Messer im*

one of the Palestinians shouts at him in Arabic, then another, then a third in English: "Hey, meester! Ball!" G continues his slow circling, holding the ball against his chest. Cohesion. The ball is oddly warm, as though it has been in the sun. Now they are screaming at him in Arabic and now they are coming after him, all twenty-two or twenty-eight of them. G talked with no one. Those who were angry were mildly angry. Others were unconcerned or cynical. American Jews—at least those with whom G spoke—were, like his wife, defensive. G could talk with

no one. Robins and mourning doves and killdeers, those stunning ring-necked plovers, highly-strung, attentive to their brood to the point of self-sacrifice. G, ball at his breast, running and sweating in the cool evening, the shrieking Arabs very close. One even shouts (G thinks) JEW! So. They've got him. They—G relinquishes the ball—

   Messer im Kopf

do it.

NOTE: *Ich hab ein glühend Messer* constitute the first line of Mahler's third song in his "Songs of a Wayfarer" cycle (1884).

134

MUSSEL

"Best represented in cool seas."

Larousse: *Animal Encyclopedia*

Q's reliable digital said eleven-twenty-eight. He saw Le Broadway Boogie, went in, sat at a small table fronting Rue des Ecoles, ordered a Calvados for nineteen francs. When he'd left his hotel near the Bastille he was thinking "Pernod," but by the time he crossed the Seine—dodging traffic, inhaling the petrol exhaust—he felt like brandy. Q had to say "Calvados" three times, first with emphasis on the second syllable, then on the first syllable, finally on the third syllable, slowly, loudly—before the waiter (old and thin with white, very dry hair) made out Q's French, slightly nodded his head.

Bad news. Mitterand diets, has his face done in Belgrade, and the franc takes a dive. So Mitterand tucks tail and sidles stiffly to the center; the franc slides further. Meanwhile, VB, the acclaimed Peruvian novelist, comes out loud and clear against the Otros. They've moved away from any "plausible revolutionary ideal"; they combine the "most virulent aspects of Stalinism and Maoism"; to "appease their insatiable power-lust, they mean to dismantle all of Peru." Thus the acclaimed VB on the notorious Otros in the esteemed (by whom?) *Atlantic Monthly*.

Eleven-forty. The appointment was for eleven-thirty. Naturally Q's contact would be late. Was there anything (outside of Mitterand's just-appointed, right-leaning, Cartesian inner-circle) that didn't get started late in Paris? First the apéritif and several Gitanes, followed by the lovemaking and bidet, followed by dinner and leisurely wine . . .

Q nursed his Calvados, ran his fingers through his thin, rain-moist hair, sneezed, sneezed again. Was the news actually bad? Was it bad that, according to the *International Herald Tribune*, the American monthly "economic index" was "up," manipulated up, so that down became up, and up meant big balls for the Senile Cowboy, big balls and another four? This wasn't necessarily bad, not at all, not dialectically. Wouldn't another four embolden the Cowboy to stick it to the poor, the un-white, the "marxist" third world? Which would, then, elasticize the Left, the fat-assed Left?

Q was thinking. In Paris he spoke French, cumbersome, execrably cadenced. He thought in English of course. He ordered another Calvados. The news, he decided, was bad and not bad. Bad in the short term for Los Otros. At least as far as getting money and matériel from French sympathizers. The Otros were used to it; they started in '58 (while Castro and Che were still in the Sierras), working to win the campesinos, establish a broad base for their revolution. To the French money-Left, the Otros resembled the M-19's of Colombia, who made guerrilla war for twenty-five years only to sign a recent wishy-washy accord with the Colombian government. The Otros weren't about to sign anything; still, they were chronic, lacked éclat, so far as the French money-Left were concerned, so Q was given to understand.

136

The waiter delivered Q's second Calvados in a small tubular goblet, with a cube of sugar. Q set the sugar cube next to the first sugar cube, sipped the Calvados, then sneezed. A woman (youngish) sat in the chair at an adjoining table, lit a Gitane, granted Q a brief smile, unfolded a copy of *Le Monde*. She ordered a Pastis from the waiter. Q's watch said eleven-fifty-three.

Q had been told the following: his contact (gender unspecified) would be in Le Broadway Boogie (Rue des Ecoles, Arrondisement 5) at eleven-thirty. Nothing more. The waiter deposited the Pastis and small carafe of water in front of the woman. She folded her *Le Monde*, sipped the cloudy liqueur, lit another Gitane, withdrew a thick paperback from her purse, opened it approximately to the middle, read. The paperback lacked a cover so that Q could not see what it was. Q ran his fingers through his hair and again he sneezed. She glanced up, no smile.

Early thirties, Q reckoned, her light brown hair fastened loosely behind her head with a wooden clasp. She displayed that peculiar French compound of severity, grace and sensuality: long-lashed clear brown eyes, high forehead, bony nose, prominent cheekbones, full flexible mouth. Slim fingers (filigreed silver band on the left forefinger, small green onyx on the right middle finger), holding the cigarette as she read.

Q sipped his Calvados. Fall '84, Paris, *Rive Gauche*, all the old savor. Except too many cars using diesel or leaded gas, the too-strong smell of exhaust even in the cafe. Q sneezed. Was the news bad for this graceful woman reading her paperback, smoking her Gitanes? Bad for her that Mrs. Gandhi murdered the Sikhs in their temple, then claimed that the temple was a warehouse for dope and dirty rupees? Or

137

did she imagine an "eternal" India, forever-flow of Ganges, excrement as light? Bad for her that the Quiche pueblo in the Guatemalan highlands was razed senselessly? Quiche women and children razed with it, senselessly? Q glanced at his watch then turned full-face to the woman, said: "Los Otros." She looked up at him, nodded, moved her chair next to his, taking her Pastis. They shook hands, her hand was cool, she applied pressure, did not immediately withdraw. "You are?" she said. "Q. Yourself?" "Moule," she said, which meant mussel. They spoke in French.

M: "Where are you staying?"
Q: "Across the river. In the fourth."
M: "Jewish quarter?"
Q: "What do you mean?"
M: "The Jewish quarter is in the fourth."
Q: "I'm staying near the Bastille."
M: Sips her Pastis. "You arrived today?"
Q: "I spent two days in Marseilles, flew here this morning."
M: "You didn't take the fast train? From Marseilles?"
Q: "No." (Sees now that the book she was reading is Rousseau's *Confessions*.)
M: "The fast train is very nice."
Q: "Ah."
(Pause)
M: "You know Peru well?"
Q: "Not well. I've travelled in it."
M: "I plan to go." Shrugs. "Someday."
(Pause)
M: "You have something for me?" Smiles. Long, shapely upper lip (like Delacroix's Liberté leading the people against Tyranny).
Q: "Yes. You want it now?"
M: "When I leave. My people will go through it tomor-

row, have an answer for you on Thursday. You can be reached at your hotel?"

Q: "Yes."

M: "I'll phone you tomorrow at eleven to set up a time for Thursday."

Q: "Evening or morning?"

M: "What? Oh—evening."

Q: "You yourself will phone?"

M: "Yes, is that good?" Small smile.

Q: "It is, yes."

M: "I hope that their response is favorable. I"—shrugs—"have nothing to do with that part."

Q: "I see."

Moule finished her Pastis and left with Q. She lived on the top-most floor of a graceful townhouse (pastel-gray, eighteenth century) just south of the river near Quai de Montebello. Three airy rooms with the original oak beams in the ceilings. Persian miniatures on the walls. They undressed and lay in the wide low bed. Moule smelled, oddly, of milk.

Untrue. They parted at Le Broadway Boogie, Q walking back over the glistening Seine. Nearly one a.m., the French still in the cafes, couples embracing in the river's shadows. Endless necklace of cars, poisonous petrol. Q tied a hand-kerchief around his nose and mouth.

A dozen different noises in Q's hotel, didn't matter, he slept well enough, up and out by eight, coffee and brioches in a nearby cafe, morning papers. Q opened the *International Herald Tribune* to the Classifieds, counted eighteen ads for "Escort Services": young "multilingual" women in Paris, London, Brussels, Geneva, Tokyo, Hong Kong, to "service you" as guide or travel companion. The phrasing of the ads homogenized, obviously a single group or consortium behind it. Q glanced at the sports, then picked up *Le Monde*.

Back in his room he phoned one of the Escort numbers in Paris. The calculatedly seductive voice (in English, French-accented) would phone back with details. Q gave his number, she returned the call, the fee was two thousand francs for the hour. Q hung up and tried another Paris number: similar voice, same protocol, same price.

Outside again, Q made two calls from a booth (neither party was in), then walked in the direction of the fifth. The exhaust made it difficult to breathe, he ducked into the Metro, out at Odeon, walking rapidly—but then pausing in front of this *clochard*: thirtyish (?), heavily bearded, face to the wall of a partially boarded-over wine store, just east of a small Norman church. The *clochard* had plastered the boarded-up walls with meticulously printed admonitions in the name—oddly—of Mormon. At least eighty (Q more or less counted them) inscriptions, each on a sheet of paper or cardboard, variously sized, up and down the walls and even on a strip of cloth wound around his head, mad beggar squatting there, head to the wall. The text, though painstakingly inscribed, was incomprehensible, evidently in the *clochard's* invented language, the single recognizable word being "Mormon." Q placed coins by the man's feet, coughed, continued walking.

To the cinema. Bresson's *Au Hasard Balthazar*. The print was blemished but the film held up well. Bresson's brave uncondescending use of the donkey. His tendency, though, to anthropomorphize. For Q, an abused donkey was an abused donkey, not an emblem of Jesus' valid suffering. Still, Q envied Bresson's dogged faith.

But didn't Q himself possess faith? Not immaterial as with Bresson. But not utterly material either. Which was, he recognized, the problem. The Otros were materialists as

140

perhaps they must be. Q's people, those working with him on the Otros' behalf, were all materialists of one stripe or another: Marxist, Marxist-Leninist, even Trotskyist (the "unceasing revolution"). Q couldn't locate himself. Was that bad? Well, it was uneasy. It promoted fantasy. It compromised one's energy. Did it? Did it compromise Moule's energy? Keen eyes and cheekbones, soft flexible mouth.

Still in the fifth, walking past the Sorbonne. Vague palimpsest here and there of the '68 wall-markings. Other walls with current markings: pro-Sinn Fein; pro-PLO; anti-Khomeini; anti-Zionist . . . The routinized Left, un-engaged, un-charged. Without charge, harmony won't issue: a dialectical axiom: the Tao of Revolution: the odd play of Q's mind.

My tongue on your shoulder. You smell, Q. whispers, of milk. Softly, she laughs. Kissing the back of your neck. Milk. Back of your thighs.

Back in the Metro, Q trained up to Montmartre, got out, walked rapidly away from the busload of German tourists, their broadbacked guide with her bullhorn. Walking up and up through the twisting cobblestone, not thinking of Toulouse-Lautrec, Modigliani, Satie, Heine: superstars, *echt*-bohemians, prismed through the infinite appropriations of *Paris-Match* . Not thinking of VB, co-generalisimo (with GM and JC) of the Latin American "magic realists," prismed through *Atlantic Monthly* as the liberal conscience of Peru, denouncing the Otros' "insatiable power-lust." Pale, tense VB, Castellano to his marrow, one long eye on the Nobel Prize.

Thinking these large things, Q, high in Montmartre, gazes over the city: stone monuments and eighteenth-century facades: impressive and consonant even with the

141

Centre Pompidou and half-dozen other anomalies and merciless petrol exhaust.

When I am in you from behind, I am at home in my skin. When I am in you, Moule, from behind, I am at home in the ridges of my skin. Swelling in you I am my blood in your skin. You are, she whispers, my revolutionary.

The pissoir was in the midst of the shopping area. Q, pausing there, could through the large air-holes watch the women and children. They in turn could see him through the same holes, his thin legs beneath the shallow covering. (Neither was inclined to see the other.) Q, like Luther in his privy, had a vision: *petite*-deviation among the French was desublimated, made redundant. Only the *grande*-deviation, as in Sade or Genet or Bataille, carried real charge. It followed that the French money-Left would have small regard for the chronic daily revolution of the Colombian M-19's or—more to the point—the Otros of Peru. Unless of course the Otros were to break big wind fast, flashily.

Back in his hotel, Q was handed a message: one of his people phoned from Amsterdam, he was to phone back. But when Q phoned there was no answer, no one on the other side. Q lay on the bed and listened to street noise; abruptly-stopping-elevator-noise;   high-heeled-footsteps-above-his-head-noise; and, from somewhere, the comfortable gurgle of a bidet: bone-warmth and shared Gitane, after *le sexe*.

Q woke to the phone. Seven-fifteen. Moule.
M: "I phoned now instead of at eleven. That all right?"
Q: "Yes."
M: "Our people have decided. Can we meet?"
Q: "Yes."
M: "At your hotel?"

Q: "Yes."

In twenty-five minutes she was in his room in her jeans and supple leather sandals; thin studded straps about the toes, another strap about the ankle. Parisian women paid strict attention to their feet. Were these called slave-shoes? Q asked.

She smiled. "Do you like them?"

"Yes. Except when I think of the skinned calf lowing at the sky."

She nodded slowly. Her eyes shone.

Q slipped off a sandal, put his lips to her slender pointed foot.

No. Q woke at six-fifty-two, coughing, lungs full of petrol from the day's walking. Washed his face, then tried to phone his people in Amsterdam. Still no response. He wondered whether the person at the desk had taken down the correct number. Earlier, riding the Metro, Q had picked up someone's abandoned *Le Figaro*. He spread it out now on the bed. On the front page, right, this headline: "Can the White Race Survive?" An "interim report" on the ongoing UNESCO-sponsored, Houston-Texas-venued conference on "People / Race / Culture." He tossed *Le Figaro* on the floor, opened *Le Monde*. On page three, a reporter, reflecting on the recent Olympics in Los Angeles, wondered why nearly all of the top sprinters were black. He said the best response he'd gotten to this question came from an old Alsatian boxing trainer: "Why? Well maybe because they don't have much time to lose in life." Q went down to dinner.

Not up to walking to Les Halles and the single vegetarian restaurant he knew, Q dined at the corner Brasserie. Fish from the Mediterranean. Carafe of Bandol rosé with the fish. Apple tart for dessert. No coffee.

Nine-eighteen, not enough time to catch a movie. Q walked toward the Place de la Bastille, the tall stone column with its crowning figure of Liberté, which looked like

Hermes, sat on a bench, watched the promenading French, at ease in their skins, smoking cigarettes, impervious to the bad air: un-cut men, pliant (thought, for them, was fluted glass, half-filled with amber); women, cheekbones rouged, soft leather sandals, bra-less, meringue panties outlined under translucent skirts or pants; but (Q still watching) what about the North African: gaunt, tense Arab or elongated Black, cut and fruitless, unabsorbed? What about the box-cars filled with cattle?

Cut Q, bent to Moule, admirably bent.

Q: *"You may not know it, but this discourse is about Parisian lingerie, about the pale arch of your foot against the stain of your sandal."*

M: *Laughs. "My revolutionary. My connoisseur of mothers."*

Q: *"I mean to revolt, Moule. Revolt in you."*

M: *"I would like us to make love in Peru."*

Q: *"The Otros pretend to love without making love. They are ascetic revolutionaries."*

M: *"I can't believe it."*

Q: *"VB says so. In the Atlantic Monthly."*

Q walking (aimlessly) among the French, the occasional North African. By the time he looked at his watch it was nearly time. Using Liberté he guided himself back to his hotel. The desk person handed him a message from Amsterdam: "Phone us immediately you hear." Q slipped the note in his pocket, went up to his room, lay on his back on the bed. The phone rang at eleven forty-eight.

Moule: "Have you seen the evening news?"

Q: "No."

M: "Two Otros hijacked a plane out of Miami en route to Caracas."

Q: "What?"

M: "They are right now in Tegucigalpa, Honduras, with the plane, a 747, and two-hundred-eighty passengers, mostly American, including the director of Voice of America. Reagan is livid."

Q: "In Honduras?"

M: "Well, they couldn't very well go to Lima." Laughs. "Can you come here?"

Q: "Now?"

M: "Now."

Q: "All right."

M: "Come. I have some good news for you."

Q took the Metro to Moule's flat off Rue St. Denis, two rooms above a *boucherie* in a red-light area. Moule called out Entrez when he knocked. She was on the phone smoking a cigarette. Q sat in the dim outer room, in a straight-backed chair. The neon lights from St. Denis made spastic patterns on the walls. The walls had nothing on them. The room contained a sofa which probably pulled out into a bed, an old square wood table, three straight-backed chairs, scattered small pillows on the crusted tile floor.

Moule continued talking on the phone, in a more or less neutral tone, apparently about a meeting she was going to the following day. She lit another cigarette. From where he sat Q could see her arms and the hand that held the cigarette, but not the phone. He saw her slender legs crossing and uncrossing. She was barefoot. Finally she hung up.

She came into the outer room carrying a bottle of Armagnac and two glasses, the cigarette in her mouth. She put the bottle and glasses on the table, went back into the other room and returned with *France-Soir*, setting it on Q's lap. On the front page toward the bottom was the story about the hijacking: Two Otros, one of whom Q knew something about, a long-time, dedicated, usually behind-the-scenes player. According to *France-Soir*, in "ironic acknowledgement" of the UNESCO conference on People / Race / Culture in Houston, Texas, the Otros first "carried out their piracy," then threatened to kill the Reagan-appointed Voice of America head unless the US government paid them six million dollars. Q put down the paper. Moule poured the Armagnac.

M: "There's been a still later development. It will be in the papers tomorrow."

Q: "Oh?"

M: "The two Otros compañeros were betrayed by the Honduran authorities and killed. US Marine sharpshooters, disguised as Honduran peasants, shot and killed the compañeros. The plane has already gone on to Caracas."

(Pause)

M: "But our people think this might have been the Otros' strategy. To project their cause in the most dramatic way possible onto the world-stage while that crazy UNESCO conference goes on in Texas."

Q: "Ah."

M: "The good news," she clinked her glass against Q's, "is that we've decided to give you what you want."

Q: "Oh."

M: "Yes. Both money and matériel."

PERSIAN LAMB

In memory of Michael Stewart

"I had elected . . . not to submit."
Richard Wright
American Hunger

Ras

Who killed 19-year-old Anthony Parchment as he was inscribing this resonant syllable with a magic marker on an IRT subway car in the Nevins Street station, 2:30 am, Thursday, mid-summer?

Who killed Frantz Fanon of French Martinique, white cells flooding his blood (black skin—white enraged cells), dreadful in Paris, dead at 36, New York City, leukemia?

From Jamaica (Westminster Parish), Anthony Parchment came to Crown Heights, Brooklyn, with his mother, two sisters. Moved in with his mother's sister, *her* three children, also from Jamaica, Kensington Parish. Anthony's Rasta father? Dead, killed with a machete by a Maroon. Maroons

147

the first Jamaican guerrillas, made it tough for the British to sip their gin, harried the Brits out in the end. Black Rasta killed by Black Maroon.

Who killed Steve Biko?

Anthony Parchment caught in the act of inscription, the talismanic *Ras*. Who beat him? The police. Who killed him? The police. The persistent reporter for the local black newspaper was told by the nurse at Bellevue Hospital that Anthony Parchment's nearly dead body arrived in the Emergency Ward manacled with four pairs of handcuffs, that he had deep bruises "all over—from the soles of his feet to his head."

Twelve days after Anthony Parchment's murder, the New York City Medical Examiner released this inquest capsule: "No indication of physical trauma. Apparent cause of death: cocaine-induced coma. Resultant heart-stoppage."

Ras. The boy got it out before they got him. It's still there, among the thousandfold graffiti, theater of the colored poor, will be there until they bury it, the subway, which is liable to be soon. Whites use busses, cars, cabs. The colored poor ride the subways, and so few bucks! bleats the City, bleats the State. We have our poor and we have our *good poor*—tell me then: who rides the subways? Who don't get the bucks? *Ras*.

"Steve Biko was shamming—he wasn't sick at all."

Anthony Parchment's mother and aunt said No to the white New York City Medical Examiner, borrowed money to hire their own pathologist, whose report confirmed what you and I know: sixty-odd bruises on his body, multiple concussions of the skull, spinal trauma, death from injuries, zero evidence of cocaine. Five weeks after these independent findings, after local black citizen outrage, the New York City Examiner revised his original report to read: "Some indication of head injury. Possibly fatal spinal trauma."

Incantatory *Ras*. Back to Ethiopia, the cradle. Cite Marcus Garvey. Worship Taffari Makonnen (Haile Selassie), Emperor of Ethiopia, Lion of Judah. Cannabis is holy (for it will grant you access). "Ital" food is holy: roots, grain, legumes, mild fruit (no meat). Away from Ethiopia looms Babylon. But while *in* Babylon, what then? Swallow? Expel? Testify? Inscribe?

And the police, the ones who beat and killed him? Three white males, ages twenty-seven to forty-one, two married with kids and living in Queens, the other living in Staten Island, all three members in good standing of the Patrolman's Benevolent Association. When asked what *Ras* meant to them, two said: "Black Power," the other said: "Black Power and heroin." When asked whether it was defensible to beat a person who was inscribing a word on the door of a subway train full of words, they refused to answer.

Who asked these things of the policemen?
I did.
Who are you?
Nobody.

You're white.
No. I mean yes.

The Parchments in Crown Heights, Brooklyn: the mother, Hyacinth, worked in a neighborhood laundromat. The two teenaged sisters went to Thomas Jefferson High School. Anthony worked in downtown Manhattan, in the garment district, maneuvering a bulky pushcart filled with mink and sable and Persian lamb from factory to showroom, back again, through the cluttered streets.

Persian lamb: the glossy black or gray pelt of the just-born (just-killed) karakul lamb with its soft tight curls. Who murdered Patrice Lumumba: his "tongue," his "nightingale breast," his "assassinated whistle"?*

All right, the boy was lynched. What now? Now, one of the three cops, the unmarried one, will be indicted for Manslaughter in the second degree, the other two will be "severely reprimanded." Manslaughter two? The indicted cop's lawyer: "If my client is guilty of anything it is of being over-zealous on the public's behalf. I feel certain that he will be totally and completely absolved of any wrongdoing whatsoever by the American judicial system and that he will never set foot in prison as an inmate." When the lawyer was asked whether Anthony Parchment's murder was significantly different from the recent lynching of a black teenager in Alabama, in which a twenty-nine-year-old white chose a black at random, cut his throat, then hung him from a tree across from his (the white man's) house, to demonstrate that the "Klan is bigger than ever in Alabama." When asked this, the lawyer actually swung at the questioner, didn't make contact.

150

You were the questioner?
Yes.
Why?
You tell me.
You're pent. All dammed up. You get off on this . . . planting.
Planting your brain-tubers. Is that it?
Not brain. No.

At his aunt's advice, Anthony Parchment cut his dreadlocks before coming to the States, thinking maybe it might
help him get a decent job. Wheeling mink and sable and
Persian lamb through the teeming streets, singing. He
didn't stop doing that. Lots of Rastas write songs, sing their
long grief. When Anthony Parchment inscribed *Ras* on the
door of the Nevins Street subway it was as a seed-syllable of
the unending song, this:

Cap-tiv-ity, Cap-tiv-ity
Youth-mon you going to die,
Dread, dread, so far from home,
Living you life in de Babylon zone,
Youth-mon you going to die.

Don't you remember what de Angel said?
De evil Somebody gonna shot you dead,
in Cap-tiv-ity, Cap-tiv-ity,
Living you life in de Babylon zone,
Dread, dread, so far from home,
Youth-mon you going to die.

Question: How is the lamb like the avant-gardist?
Answer: Both are granted a window ledge on the city's
outskirts and a single line of elegaic prose in an interior page

151

of the medium newspaper. Later—much later—their horny carapace is exhumed, liveried, displayed to distracted mild applause.

And you? Are your post-mortems, your abracadabra witnessing, any different? Your cubist musings? Your doleful celebrations of martyrdom? Your moony "history"? Your thinly-veiled self-pity? Your spleen in lamb's clothing?

Right, he had a girlfriend, Mattie Taylor, born in Trinidad, also living in Brooklyn with her family. She sings. Anthony would write the songs, the two of them would sing them, that was their goal. Poor young people—especially it seems, non-white young—speak of goals. Middle-class young speak of desk-calendars, agendas, careers—there's a difference. It's not over yet but the cop's lawyer was right: his client'll get off, no big deal.

Motive? I mean Anthony Parchment's motive for doing what he did where he did it, when. Could be he wanted a taste of what it feels like: write songs people feel; add his bit to the hundreds on the door, thousands, tens of thousands of colored inscriptions in the Underground. Scrawls, signs, totems, verses, signatures, ideograms, self-portraits. That hot, hot moist a.m., with its third-rail and litter and sharp sour smells of fermenting soda pop and fast-food mustard and sweat from the endless work-a-day and gutted phones and cavernous rumblings, darkness. Could be he wanted to testify to the power of the word. *Ras.* Didn't his father die for it? Weren't the lambs marooned in Babylon because of it? Could be he was restless and didn't really want to think of maneuvering the bulky cart full of pungent pelts through the cluttered streets, not want to think.

Together, Anthony Parchment and Mattie Taylor did what teenagers do: caress, couple, laugh, flirt. More: sing Anthony's songs; also Anthony taught her *Ras;* smoked herb, learned *Ras.* That's right. *Ras* ain't only for Jamaicans but for uprooted Blacks anywhere.

The oldest cop had been the brutal one, using his club in the subway; in the radio car using the heel of his hand; in the police station kicking with his black, thick-soled shoes. Only once did their eyes squarely meet, thin black young man / bulky red-haired cop, and Anthony recognized him from his dream, in which his father was being beaten by such a man, white with red hair, *but made-up to look black,* beaten with his fists, not fighting back, then with the machete, slashed hard with the machete, and then the killer saw him, Anthony, running through the white-faced choir, white small teeth, white chins pointed down like daggers, and the killer gaining on him when he willed himself to wake, and this dream was dreamed in Jamaica but he never forgot his assassin's face.

Not him, the oldest cop with red hair, but the youngest, least brutal (maybe) of the three, the unmarried one, was the only one actually charged: Manslaughter 2, since—it was reasoned—he had the least to lose, no family, no property, just two years on the force, and ballsy too, didn't know fear, besides the lawyer would get him off so no big deal, and as a bonus they'd change his duty, move him out of Nevins Street, Brooklyn, give him Manhattan's Upper East Side.

The third cop, age thirty-three, a lanky tall man with prematurely gray hair and a lot of tattoos, a wife, three young daughters, a small house in Corona, Queens, went to Avia-

153

tion High School, wanted to be a plane mechanic, worked instead for Chevrolet, tried for the fire fighters but failed the test, tried twice for the cops, made it, was real gung-ho, killed a black teenager once before while driving his patrol car on a call, got off that one easy too, they transferred him to Transit.

Hyacinth Parchment refused to be interviewed. Anthony Parchment's aunt said only: "Anthony loved to laugh. He would put his head back and just laugh. I can hear it in my head."

Why was Steve Biko arrested?

Sedition.

Why was he manacled to his cell at Walmer Police Station?

To prevent his escape.

And why was he kept naked in his cell at Walmer Police Station?

To prevent self-inflicted death.

How is it that Steve Biko suffered severe brain damage?

He was presented with his comrades' written testimony naming him as the leader of the attempted violent sedition. When he read this unassailable evidence he banged his head against the wall in frustration.

And the numerous deep bruises on his body?

Any bruises would have been self-inflicted. The prisoner had been a medical student and was utterly familiar with yoga.

How would you justify transporting the brain-injured and battered Steve Biko, naked, on the floor of a truck, one thousand kilometers to Pretoria?

The trip was necessary to administer the spinal tap to ascertain the extent of the prisoner's brain damage. It was determined that the prisoner stood a better chance of surviving the journey than surviving otherwise.

You were wrong?
Not necessarily.
(Steve Biko was buried outside King Williams Town, near the small dusty township where he had grown up. He was thirty years old.)

Anthony Parchment's family and friends sat in the back of the airless courtroom in witness of the proceedings that found the indicted police officer innocent of Manslaughter and his case dismissed after a judicial reprimand. As the three officers and their families, grinning, clapping each other on the back, filed from the courtroom, a white bystander stood up and shouted: "Sham! Sham! No black person will ever get justice in this whitened sepulcher, this rich man's cess!"

The white—thin, dark-haired, middle-aged—was forcibly restrained (by two of the formerly-accused officers), then held in contempt. Hyacinth Parchment witnessed the white man's outburst with the same (nearly expressionless) disapproval with which she had witnessed the court proceedings.

It was you who made the outburst.
Yes.
To what end?
Don't talk to me of ends. I'm not the keeper of accounts.

Like promised, the let-off cop got off his bad duty in Nevins Street and was transferred to the Upper East Side. He also got engaged to his high-school sweetheart and made plans to move from Staten Island, in fact, put a downpayment on a small brick house in the northeast Bronx, closer to his new duty. Have you ever been in the northeast Bronx? It's white and clean and Roman Catholic and surprisingly wooded with numerous species of birds but almost no mammals. Except for rats and mice, the homeowners pretty much hunted down all the mammals, ate the ones that were edible, stripped the pelts from the ones that were valuable.

Who killed Marcus Garvey?
Ras, it ain't easy.

* Roberto Armijo, "To Patrice Lumumba," in *Volcán: Poems from El Salvador, Guatemala, Honduras, Nicaragua* (City Lights, 1983), pp. 26-27. Translated by David Volpendesta.